ONCE THERE WERE STACKS
OF THEM

ONCE THERE WERE STACKS OF THEM

OF THEM

Stories of Stockport's Last Chimney Premises

By

BERNARD HAYES

REWORD PUBLISHERS

2004

Published by
REWORD PUBLISHERS
3 Syddal Crescent
Bramhall
Cheshire SK7 1HS

www.reword.co.uk

ISBN 0 9536743 9 8

Printed and Bound by
Gopsons Papers
India

This book is dedicated to
my wife, Edwina,
who had to endure the despair I showed with my P.C.
as I struggled through the layout stage.

I thank her wholeheartedly for encouraging me to see it through.

About the Author

Bernard Hayes spent his career in engineering, the last 30 years of it in Stockport. Although born and raised in London he comes from past generations of Lancastrians, but married a Lincolnshire girl, and they have three children all born in Cheshire. It was only when all the children had left home and retirement set in that he began to research his surroundings, starting with the brown field site where he lives that was once a bleach works. This expanded into other sites of industrial and commercial interest and the research culminated with the compilation of this book.

ACKNOWLEDGEMENTS

In addition to those people mentioned under the headings of "Information Sources", to whom I am most grateful for the help I have received, I particularly wish to thank the team of librarians at Stockport Heritage Library who always managed to produce some form of record about a subject of my choice. A special thank you to David Reid, not only for allowing me to reproduce illustrations held in the local history section of Stockport Central Library, but also for his general advice and initial encouragement to persevere with this project. The hand drawn maps were constructed by the author after studying the A to Z for Greater Manchester and Ordnance Survey maps for each locality. The colour photographs were also taken by the author, but the black and white photograph (page 26) is reproduced by courtesy of Stockport Local History Library. I also wish to thank Messrs. Buckleys (Printers), Deanprint Ltd. and Park & Paterson Ltd. for approving the inclusion of their respective logos. Finally I apologise for any omitted or incorrect references to people or places. Those made are believed to be accurate.

ONCE THERE WERE STACKS OF THEM

Stories of Stockport's Last Chimney Premises

By

Bernard Hayes

Contents

INTRODUCTION

"The town is well paved, and the principal part of it is built of brick on steep and irregular hills of soft red sandstone, rising in some places precipitously from the banks of the Mersey..........The situation of Stockport gives it at all times a picturesque appearance; and at night when the factories are lighted up, the view is exciting in the extreme."

Such was the description (in part) of Stockport in the 1880's in the *National Encyclopaedia* of the day. One could claim it is equally striking today with the illuminated viaduct and pyramid building, but certainly not from factories. Like many northern industrial towns, Stockport once possessed a skyline dominated by factory chimneys. Slowly they have nearly all disappeared – few indeed to be seen in the centre of town. Where there was a chimney one could guarantee that something of a substantial nature was taking place there and it was not necessarily the practice of a cotton mill as the following pages will show. This book describes those premises with chimneys that survived into the 1990's, their functions and some of the town's personalities that were associated with them.

CHIMNEY CONSTRUCTION

Wherever there is a boiler a tall chimney of some kind is necessary to carry away the products of combustion. In addition, a chimney is a means of producing draught caused by the difference in temperature and therefore the density, between a hot column of gas in the chimney and a similar column of cold air outside the chimney. Consequently the taller the chimney the greater the draught, but a chimney alone is not the most efficient way of producing draught and today both forced and induced draught fans are utilised to obtain complete combustion and minimum pollution.

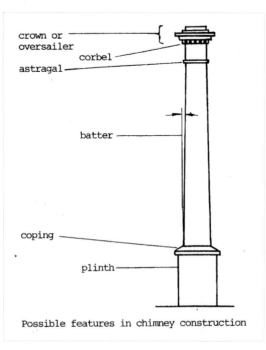

Possible features in chimney construction

chimney was built taller than their neighbour's chimney purely for the prestige it gave them. However there were guidelines for calculating both the height and cross sectional area for a chimney based on the consumption of coal. For example the *Mechanical World* Diary and Year Book for 1917 indicated that for a consumption of 100 tons of coal per week of 56 hours the design chimney height should be 180 ft. This not only tells us the height for a typical chimney of that period but also provides us with an insight into some of the conditions prevailing at the time, like the length of the working week. All the early chimneys were brick built with an internal lining of firebrick, a cavity separating the lining from the outer shell. Usually they were narrower at the top than at the bottom, the taper referred to as "batter". Some chimneys were set upon a plinth and some were also topped with a projecting crown called the oversailer that assisted the dispersal of smoke. A few chimneys were constructed from concrete blocks, but most of the modern chimneys consist of a parallel steel tube from which one may never see the emission of smoke, such is the efficiency of the gas or oil fired boilers that now exist.

In the days of coal burning when most of the early chimneys were erected, the height of chimneys was regulated by local conditions including any by-laws that may have existed. Surroundings such as high buildings or hills causing baffling currents of air would also be taken into account. In populous districts it was said to be desirable to have a chimney of not less than 75ft. high. Quite often chimneys up to this height would be square in section but the taller ones were either octagonal or round in section. As a very rough guide octagonal chimneys belong to the 19th century and round chimneys belong to the 20th century. It was alleged that some mill owners ensured their

Location Map

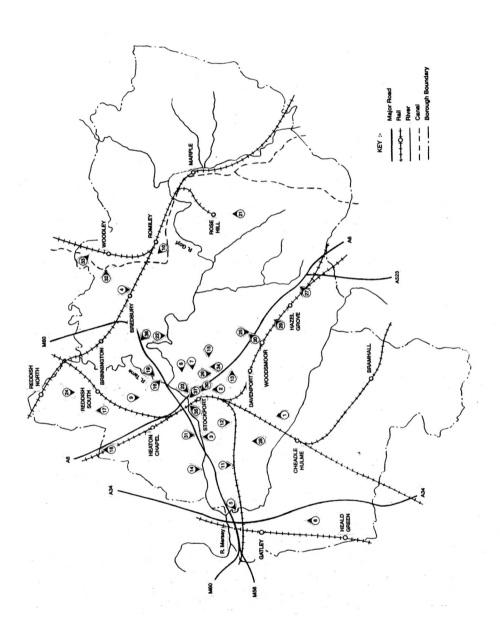

KEY :-
— Major Road
— Rail
— River
— Canal
— Borough Boundary

Adswood Brickworks

O.S.ref. SJ886 877

The making of bricks has been carried out in the Adswood area since the 1870's, thanks to the presence of a series of clay pits located on the south side of Garners Lane and Adswood Road. The Adswood Tile Works was operating west of *The Greyhound* pub in 1882, whereas the present day site, east of *The Greyhound*, was merely designated "Brickfield" on the Cheadle Hulme and District O.S.map of 1882. A third site was also in existence in the early 1900's about 2 miles further east called The Davenport Brick and Tile Co. This latter site was subsequently landscaped to become the original Davenport Golf Course, but even that eventually gave way for housing and a school, the golf club relocating to Higher Poynton.

One of the earliest names in brick making locally was that of Alexander Burslam who was known to have been making bricks at Adswood Road between 1882 and 1887, but one cannot be sure if he operated east or west of *The Greyhound*. Certainly by 1898 the site east of The Greyhound was well established and this came to be known as The Adswood Brick and Tile Works. It was not until 7th April 1922 however that a corporate company was set up, when two families (the Harrison's and the Jackson's) formed the brick making firm of J & A Jackson, with Joseph Jackson as its first chairman. Joseph Jackson was related to the Harrison family by marriage and although the business carried his name, it was the Harrison Family that really formed the backbone of the company. There were seven brothers from the Harrison family who either managed or worked in the various works that the company acquired around Manchester and district in the early 1900's. J & A Jackson Ltd. set up their original headquarters at their Pink Lane site in Longsight, then to Swinton in 1974 and finally to Adswood. The Jackson family fell out with the board and subsequently retired from the business in 1935 but the name of the company remained intact for another 50 years.

One of the requirements associated with brickmaking is the acquisition of suitable clay-bearing land, which is why so many sites were owned by J & A Jackson all around North West England. Another requirement, often stipulated as a condition, is the disposal of worked-out land. At Adswood the worked-out land was sold to Greater Manchester Waste Disposal Authority for back filling. This in turn resulted in the generation of methane gas that could at times, if the calorific value was high enough,

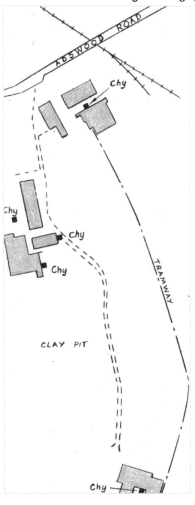

Distribution of 5 chimneys as shown on the O.S. map for 1910

provide a back-up fuel for firing the kilns. Today one will see only one chimney at Adswood, a square section structure approximately 115ft. high built in 1928. In 1934 there were as many as five chimneys, one for each kiln, which in those days were chamber kilns where bricks were baked in batches and the side of the kilns walled up each time a firing took place. It is a reflection of the new technology employed in brick making today that only one chimney is necessary as the present day kiln is described as a tunnel kiln allowing for continuous processing. The fuel used to fire the kilns has progressed over the years from coal, oil, and liquid propane to North Sea gas. On the O.S. map for 1934 one can see that five chimneys were in use shared between three separate groups of buildings. The buildings were also linked by a tramway and the buildings nearest Adswood Road were also served by a railway siding that branched off the New Mills and Heaton Mersey Line Railway. Use of the railway ceased in 1968 in favour of road transport.

In the 1970's the company was subjected to several take-over offers and eventually one from Christian Salvesen was accepted, the company changing hands on 5th December 1973, but the name did not change from J & A Jackson Ltd. to Salvesen Brick Ltd. until June 1986. Christian Salvesen, a Norwegian company, was renowned in the 1950's for its fleet of whaling ships – diversification indeed. Later Christian Salvesen decided to sell the brick making company and in March 1995 a management buy-out resulted in a change in the company name to Chelwood Brick, reflecting the firm's location on Adswood Road but adjacent to Cheadle. To mark the 75th anniversary of brick making at this site the company produced a souvenir booklet entitled *Chelwood Brick – a tradition of excellence*. It now manages four sites scattered across the country, one of which (Sandown Works, Aldridge, Staffordshire) is considered to be run by means of the most advanced technology for brick making in the world, having an output in excess of 5 million bricks per year. After yet another merger in 2002 the company has been called *The Brick Business*.

Information Sources:- booklet *Chelwood Brick- a tradition of excellence*
O.S.maps for 1872,1898,1910 and 1934
Wayne Richards of Chelwood Brick

T.W.Bracher & Co.

O.S.ref. SJ895 894

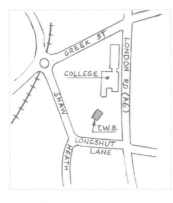

These premises were originally built around 1870 as a hat factory for Messrs. Sutton and Torkington who had moved to a much larger purpose built factory. In 1879 a Mr.T.W.Bracher established a company in Higher Hillgate for making hatboxes, later moving to Waterloo Road, and then once again into the premises in Royal George Street vacated by Sutton and Torkington in 1898. They have remained there to this day and became known for their manufacture of hat trimmings such as cap peaks, hat leathers, gold blocking and label printing. Around the 1900's there was a brief tie-up between Mr.Bracher and Joseph Dean (the founder of Deanprint Ltd.), but an infringement of patent rights brought their association to an end. T.W.Bracher was an inventive man and became notable for his development of a machine for sewing the edge of hat leathers, a process that became known throughout the hatting trade as "brachering". He also developed a remarkable machine to make bowler hat wires. This machine would automatically form wire into an oval shape, curved from front to back and cut it off to any given size. These wires were produced in their millions and around 100 people were employed when production was at its peak. Their export business was extensive.

It is believed that the square section chimney was erected at the same time as the original building, as the hatting process would have required substantial quantities of steam from an equally substantial boiler. In the late 1800's a gas engine was installed powering line shafting throughout the works and at that time the chimney was used for a central heating boiler. During the 1920's Thomas Hart of T.W.Bracher & Co. installed a diesel generator from an ex World War 1 submarine and individually motorised most of the equipment. The generator was retained for some years, in case of emergency, and came to the rescue (in times of power cuts in the public supply system) by supplying electricity to one of the neighbours – St.Thomas's Hospital.

ESTABLISHED 1879

SUPPLIERS OF HAT & CAP LEATHERS,
CAP PEAKS, CHIN STRAPS,
STIFFENERS, BOWS, etc., etc.
to Home & Overseas
Markets

Telephone :
STO 2005

Telegrams :
"BRACHER, STOCKPORT"

T. W. Bracher & Co. Ltd.
Royal George Street,
Stockport.

EMBOSSING
PRINTING
HAT LABELS, etc.

LEATHER STITCHING

Advert from the 1949 edition of the Stockport Official Handbook

A view taken from the direction of Shaw Heath

Information Sources:- *Stockport History Trail* – Stockport Education Authority
Yesteryears – A History of Deanprint Ltd.
J.M.Chatterton of T.W.Bracher & Co. Ltd.

Brinksway Leather Works

O.S.ref. SJ879 899

There was once a number of industrial concerns on Higher Brinksway including Gorsey Bank Doubling Mill and Samuel Moorhouse's Brinksway Bank Mill, but the only one to survive into the 21st century was the one time leather works with the confusing addresses of either Gorsey Bank, Higher Brinksway or sometimes No.2 Stockport Road. This confusion partly came about because the works was situated right on the Stockport/Cheadle Heath border and each authority listed the leather works in its directory in a different way.

In his book *Industrial Archaeology of Stockport*, Owen Ashmore describes the Brinksway Leather Works as one of the later tanneries to be set up in Stockport mentioning that it was on an O.S. map of 1895. However another map indicates that the rear part of the premises (that nearest the river Mersey) was present in 1872 and the owner at the time of writing (Mr. E. Ablett) believes the works date from earlier than that. The first written evidence of ownership, gained from the Stockport trade directories is that of Tom Cocker, junior, who moved into the Brinksway Leather Works in 1887, having previously practised at a leather works in St.Petersgate. Tom Cocker, like his father before him, produced hat leathers and was described at one stage as a "Hat, Cap, and Fancy Leather Manufacturer". He lived in Chatham Street, Edgeley in the early 1900's and later became a director of the Palmer Mills Co.

The building consisted of three storeys, brick built with a hipped slate roof. Unusually the chimney emerged through a valley in the roof thereby belying its true height that was probably about 80ft tall. Round in section the chimney was used during the tannery period of the works when an extensive amount of steam cleaning of leather would have been undertaken. Tom Cocker's leather works remained in business until 1962 after which time the chimney laid dormant, deteriorating with the weather and supporting plant life until it was capped off at roof level in 2001.

It is possible that the occupier of the works prior to Tom Cocker was Thomas Orme who was principally a Billiard Table Maker. However he was also a tanner by trade with a Higher Brinksway address between 1872 and 1887, and so may well have used these same premises.

The occupier after Tom Cocker was the company of C.W.Eayrs Ltd. who moved into the Brinksway Works in 1964/5 from Mersey Square. They were Motor Component Distributors and remained at the Brinksway premises for the next 20 years. Their name still remains in large white letters on the east wall of the building. The premises were later purchased by Eric Ablett (a property dealer) who used part of the building for his own workshop and rented other sections out to various businesses. Some of these were wrought-iron fabricators, a joinery company, and motor vehicle repairers.

Information Sources :-   Stockport Trade Directories 1872 to 1938
                            Eric Ablett

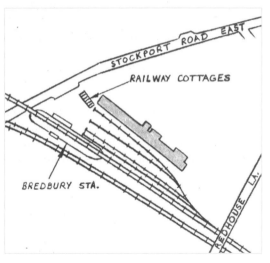

The long shed as depicted on the O.S. map for 1910

BTR Vitaline, Bredbury

O.S. ref. SJ929 918

The unpretentious buildings on this site were once the home to three widely different practices, the first one connected with the railways, although to what use it was put remains uncertain. It was around the end of the 19th century that the long shed was built alongside the goods yard adjacent to Bredbury Railway Station on the Great Central and Midland Joint Railway. This particular stretch of rail, opened in August 1875, was, in railway terms, one of the later constructions to take place in the Manchester District. The photograph taken from the station shows part of the 100 yard long shed in front of which one can see the station car park of today (2000). In earlier years this was the goods yard – a busy operation with four sidings. In the bottom left corner of the photograph the beer garden for *The Rising Sun* pub is just visible backing on to railway cottages. Beyond these cottages there are several buildings and a chimney that were believed to have been erected around 1924/5 when the Hyde and District Cooperative Ltd. took over the site for use as a laundry. The round chimney (about 50ft. high to the top of the brickwork) was in the style of the period and would have been a necessity to support a boiler for all the hot water and steam required in laundering. No doubt the proximity of the railway goods yard was advantageous for the supply of coal for the boilers. Hyde and District Launderers Association Ltd. carried on business at Bredbury until 1952/3 but then transferred to Broadstone Hall Road, Reddish. A year later the third and final type of business was set up when Redferns Rubber, of Hyde, moved in. The firm became known as Redferns (Bredbury) Ltd. In 1969 British Vita took over the company, renaming it Vitamol (Clyde) Ltd.

Finally, following a merger between British Vita and BTR Ltd. of Leyland in 1973, it became BTR Vitaline Ltd. BTR stood for British Tyre Rubber and they had been engaged in rubber lining since the 1920's. The new company became one of the largest in the United Kingdom to be involved in designing rubber linings against chemical attack. Their expertise was in applying linings and coverings of both hard and soft, natural and synthetic rubber to all types of vessels, ducting and pipework both on site and in their factory. In order to cure the rubber after lining it was necessary to place the rubber lined equipment (where size allowed) into a steam heated autoclave. And so the boiler plant was again necessary to raise steam during this third phase of the site's history. The chimney height was raised during this period by a further 10ft. or so by inserting a steel tube up the centre of the chimney. By this time the brickwork of the chimney had been heavily strapped both vertically and circumferentially.

According to an article in the *Stockport Express/Advertiser* of 19th February 1981, a time when the company had a workforce of 60, it was explained that "Vita" meant *life* and linked with "line" suggested *lifeline.* But it would need more than these sentiments to sustain the future of the business because the demand for rubber lining diminished as more and more corrosive resistant materials such as glass fibre and some of the reinforced plastics were surviving corrosive environments. This resulted in a lean order book for BTR Vitaline and after the 1980's the company struggled to survive. The company closed in February 1999, 28 people losing their jobs. By the autumn of 1999 the premises had been sold and demolition contractors were preparing to clear the site in readiness for a housing development.

BTR Vitaline polymeric linings and coverings provide contamination-free protection against acids and plating solutions, abrasive or corrosive chemicals, organic materials and inorganic salts and alkalis. BTR Vitaline linings and coverings can be applied to almost any type of plant. If you have a chemical plant lining problem, contact us immediately.

BTR VITALINE LIMITED
Stockport Road, Bredbury, Cheshire. Tel: 061-430 2687

a vital part of the engineering and chemical industries

Advert from the Stockport Official Handbook 1976

Information Source :- *Stockport Official Handbook 1976*

Cheadle Lower Mill

O.S.ref. SJ855 890

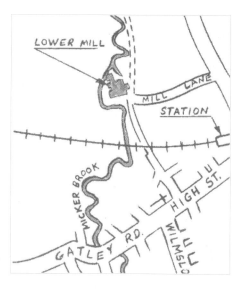

Cheadle in the 1950's

There must have been hundreds of roads all over England and Wales called Mill Lane but few perhaps that lead to a mill with such a tranquil rural setting as the one by the side of the *Micker Brook* north of Cheadle. This was originally the site of the manorial mill of Cheadle Bulkeley, there being another mill on the south side of the same brook called Cheadle Higher Mill that served the manor of Cheadle Moseley. Compared with Higher Mill there is relatively little written about Cheadle Lower Mill. It served the manor of Cheadle Bulkeley as early as the 14th century and by 1784 was known to have had five pairs of grinding stones. The earliest known occupier was Elizabeth Jowett, who, in 1834, is recorded as a corn miller. Her son William took over some years later being recorded in the 1851 census as a corn miller employing 4 men. Also residing at the mill was his wife and mother (then age 64), and two servant girls. The Jowett family ran the mill for a good 20 years but by 1872 appeared to have abandoned it. By that time a 20 horse-power steam engine had been installed to supplement the existing water power estimated at 50 horse power.

The next occupant was William Mosley, junior, who, in about 1878, set up a bleaching business there. The site became known as Cheadle Bleach Works. He had an office at 28 Brown Street in Manchester but ten years later the Manchester office was at 85 Mosley Street. In keeping with most of the bleaching companies in and around Manchester the firm of William Mosley became a member of the Bleachers Association as did Sykes & Co. of Edgeley and Melland & Coward of Heaton Mersey. The presence of water in the *Micker Brook* and a weir to provide a head of water for power must have been a real asset for a bleach works, though later it is understood that the council for Cheadle put pressure on factory owners to use less water. By way of encouragement the Council offered to build the chimney if the owner installed a larger steam plant. Such chimneys were known as "compensation chimneys". The one at Cheadle Lower Mill was built round in cross-sections to a height of about 100ft.

Bleaching ceased at the Mill Lane works around 1938 and two other companies later occupied the premises. The first was the Croft Laundry Co. Ltd. that was there during the 1940's, the other being The Standard Chemical Co., a firm founded by the Horsfield Brothers for manufacturing and supplying detergents to the textile industry. James and Albert Horsfield, both accomplished lacrosse players, built up a thriving business that in 1978 had a workforce of 50 people. However, in 1991 when the company was taken over by Thor Chemicals, the workforce had been reduced to 27. To mark this change of ownership the new Managing Director, Mr. Barry Horsfield, enlisted the services of the well-known Bolton steeplejack Fred Dibnah to scale the chimney and change the name from *Standard* to *Thor.* This took place in March 1992, but the chimney was no longer in use after that except for advertising the company. Thor Chemicals Ltd., who originally set up locally in Reddish, decided to relocate to a larger site in Cheadle Hulme and so the Mill Lane factory closed in 1995. Sadly the buildings at Cheadle Lower Mill have deteriorated badly since they were vacated, with most of the roofing gone exposing one of the two Lancashire boilers sitting on its cradle.

Advert from
The Cheadle and Gatley Handbook 1970

Information Sources:-
The Changing Functions of the Village of Cheadle, Cheshire by Stuart Hilton.
Cheadle library

Cheadle Royal Hospital

O.S.ref. SJ853 866

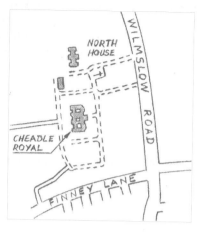

The location on Wilmslow Road of Cheadle Royal Hospital is well known to the majority of local people, but they will probably not be aware of the neat group of outbuildings partially hidden by trees to the north west of the main building. It is here that one finds the chimney that formed part of the power house providing gas (later electricity) and hot water for hospital use.

Cheadle Royal, on this site, dates back to 1847 but one must go back to 1763 to trace the roots of this mental institution. The Manchester Royal Infirmary (located just off Piccadilly) had been established 11 years when in 1763 the Board of Trustees met "to consider of a proper Plan to provide for and cure such Patients as are disordered in their senses". As a result of this meeting a committee was appointed which in turn recommended a "Hospital for Lunaticks" for the reception of in-patients, such hospital to be controlled under the same management as the infirmary. It was the admission of *in-patients* that would herald the beginning of proper mental care. The general scene in the mid 1700's was one of poorhouses, the gaol or the private madhouse, the latter demanding extortionate fees and often taking in persecuted sane victims. In all of these alternatives there would have been no attempt at separating the sane from the lunatic.

Parliament approved Manchester's proposal and shortly after a fund was established to build a hospital. Donations came flooding in headed by 100 guineas from a Mr. William Wright, gentleman of Stockport, with the result that the *Manchester Lunatick Hospital* was opened on 10th May 1766, becoming the third only hospital in England to admit mental patients. By 1820 the hospital had the capability of treating over 100 patients, but the site had become built up and noisy, and the buildings, in spite of several extensions, had become hopelessly out of date. Compared to many County Asylums that had by then been set up, Manchester's hospital did not fare well. However the treatment it offered was considered to rank amongst the best available and had nothing to fear from the Madhouse Act that had been passed in 1828 in order to regulate the running and inspection of mental hospitals. This situation eventually led to the purchase of some 37 acres of land at Cheadle for the purpose of building a new hospital with accommodation for not less than 70 patients. Building commenced and within three years the new hospital opened in 1850 as *The Manchester Royal Hospital for the Insane* retaining that title until 1902 when it became *Cheadle Royal Hospital*. During its early years Cheadle Royal had a rough passage, suffering from poor attendance and low income, but high costs mostly associated with the maintenance of its extensive grounds. It was due largely to the efforts of Dr. Henry Maudsley (the Medical Superintendent appointed in 1859), that Cheadle Royal's fortunes turned. After Dr. Maudsley's short but effective reign, there followed a period of real expansion, gaining for Cheadle Royal the reputation of a caring hospital and known for its innovative schemes for treating suitable patients in home surroundings outside the main building. The medical Superintendent over this period was Dr. George William Mould who held the position for 41 years and was said to have "made" the hospital.

Of all the extensions one of the major additions was the building of *North House* in 1903 to accommodate another 100 patients. In 1959 Cheadle Royal Industries Ltd. was set up. This was intended as a rehabilitation unit for making such things as paper hats, disposable paper bags, confetti, and rosettes all labelled "Cheeri" – their brand name. This has been most successful and has been widely admired and imitated. At one time the grounds for Cheadle Royal Hospital extended to 280 acres.

The site of the Power House has its own history, starting with the need for water. In the early years of medical treatment there was a genuine belief in the curative effects of taking regular baths and so Cheadle Royal ensured it was self sufficient in this matter. Water was supplied from a reservoir (marked on the O.S.map for 1872), filtered and pumped up, by means of a steam engine, to several cisterns mounted on the roof. Heating of the water was also by steam generated from what was described as a 14 horsepower boiler. There was also a gas works on this site that presumably supplied the early lighting system. All of this was sourced from coal at 12s 2d per ton (1852 prices). In the early 1890's gas lighting was replaced by electricity generated from Cheadle Royal's own dynamos. The boiler house left standing today was built in the first quarter of the 20th century to provide hot water and steam for the laundry as well as space heating to the buildings. This was no small undertaking as can be seen in the size of the boiler house and 80ft. chimney. Around 1990 they were shut down and replaced in favour of the installation of modern boilers in individual buildings.

Following the formation of the National Health Service in 1948, Cheadle Royal severed its links with Manchester Royal Infirmary and became independent, remaining so to the present time and now managed by Cheadle Royal Healthcare Ltd. In the 1960's someone had a grand vision for Cheadle Royal as a comprehensive health neighbourhood that included a hamlet for the aged and a 600-bed hospital. This never materialised. Now, in the 21st century, the activities at Cheadle Royal have been condensed within 23 acres, the land outside its boundaries, including North House, being developed as a business park.

The more usual view of Cheadle Royal

Information Sources:- *A Short History of Cheadle Royal* by Edward M Brockbank
Cheadle Royal Hospital- a bicentenary history by Nesta Roberts
Director of Business Development – Cheadle Royal Healthcare Ltd.

Christys' Hat Works

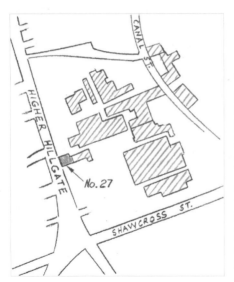

O.S.ref. SJ899 898

There was only a slender modern steel chimney to complement the factory at Christys' by the 1990's, but no account of Stockport's past would be complete without the story of this important company that once produced hats for all parts of the world. The history of Christys' has been well documented, the basic story commencing in 1773 when a Quaker by the name of Miller Christy established a hat-making firm in London. As the business of this firm (Christy & Co.) grew, several provincial firms were commissioned to make hats for the London company. One such provincial firm was that of Thomas and John Worsley who had been making hats at their Canal Street works in Stockport since the 1790's. In 1826 the Worsleys retired so the business and premises at Canal Street were taken over by Christys' for the manufacture of all types of wool and fur hat. This became Christy's production centre in the north of England.

Concurrently with the above, a businessman called Samuel Oldknow came to Stockport from Chorley, purchasing a dwelling house and a warehouse in Higher Hillgate in 1784. Both the house (number 27), that still stands, and the warehouse, occupied part of the site now being described. Oldknow soon got down to developing the site by building a new factory and became the first Stockport mill owner to install steam power. However he over-reached himself and became bankrupt but was fortunately saved by Richard Arkwright who accepted part of the Hillgate property as settlement of Oldknow's debt. Thereafter the premises were owned by a succession of different industrialists until Christy's bought the site in 1844.

The Christy factory with No.27 Higher Hillgate to the right

For a while Christys' carried on their hat production at Canal Street, letting out the Hillgate mill to cotton manufacturers. Whilst the Christy family were in Stockport they used the house at No.27 Higher Hillgate as their residence. Eventually as the business developed, land was purchased between Canal Street and Higher Hillgate until the site covered about 11 acres. By the 1880's South Mill had been built and an engraving of that time illustrated chimneys at Canal Street, Hillgate and South Mill. Also by this time Oldknow's former house, no longer the Christy family residence, had become the factory offices. The Hillgate Mill chimney was rebuilt in 1882, being octagonal on a square plinth, 105 ft. tall, and designed by John West of Manchester. This chimney served the boiler house and various kilns within the mill via exhaust flues. It was believed to have been in use until the 1940's but only the square base survived up to 1996. Another building was erected in 1882 and further extended 10 years later following destruction of the first Hillgate Mill by fire. They called this building Victoria Mill but its use was primarily for warehousing rather than manufacturing. On completion it was one of the longest buildings on the site measuring 77 by 12 metres.

The hatting industry reached its peak in the first decade of the twentieth century, Christys' alone employing 1500 people at Hillgate. However following World War 1 there was a steady decline in the industry, initiated by overseas countries setting up their own industries and thereby reducing the market for British exports. There was a further decline after World War 2 and in 1953 Christys' bought out the Stockport hatting firms of Lincoln Bennett, Henry Heath, Tress, Scotts and Chestergate Hat Manufacturing. In that year they closed both their manufacturing and office headquarters in London and centred everything at Stockport. Then in 1964 Christys' took over the Stockport firm of Sutton and Torkington, well known for their speciality of velour as well as felt hats. The remaining hat manufacturers in the Stockport area decided to amalgamate and thus the Associated British Hat Manufacturers Ltd. was formed in 1966. This comprised Christy & Co., Battersby & Co., T & W Lees Ltd., from Stockport and the two firms of Joseph Wilson & Sons Ltd. and J Moores & Sons Ltd. from Denton. Although some names from the past were retained, only Christys' and Wilsons continued to manufacture, the rest closing.

Christys' trade mark first registered in
March 1876

Of the Christy family, three deserve a mention for their contributions to society. *Wakefield* Christy was the great grandson of the founder and for a while (after marrying in 1872) lived as a tenant at Bramall Hall. He became a wealthy man after acquiring estates left by his uncle Samuel, and in the 1890's donated 5 acres of land to make possible the building of St. George's Church in Heaviley. Wakefield spent a lot of his time in Ireland and became High Sheriff of County Down, where he died in 1898 as Wakefield Christy-Miller. This change of name came about in 1890 and was arranged by Royal Licence.

Wakefield's fifth child, *Geoffry*, was born in 1881, joined the hatting firm in 1905 and became a director in 1911. Geoffry strengthened the link his father made with St. George's Church by marrying the eldest daughter of the vicar, Archdeacon Thorpe. He served in World War One with the Ox. And Bucks. Light Infantry and was awarded the Military Cross in 1916. In 1918 he became Lt.Col. of 2/5th Battalion of the Gloucester Regiment. After the war he became chairman of the Stockport War Memorial Fund raising £24,000 for the building of the town's war memorial. He was also chairman of Swain & Co. from 1950 to 1961 and chairman of the board of governors of Stockport Grammar School in 1950. Additionally he had a long association with Stockport Infirmary being its treasurer for 30 years. In 1947 he was appointed Deputy Lieutenant of the County of Cheshire. In recognition of such notable public service, particularly for his services with the Cheshire Branch of the Territorial Army, (for which he had been chairman from 1943 to 1950), he was awarded the K.C.B. in 1951. Sir Geoffry died age 88 years in 1969 leaving a son *John* (his eldest) who had similarly distinguished himself.

Known as Lt.Col. Christy-Miller, John had served with the Cheshire Regiment throughout the Second World War. In 1965 he was elected Chairman of the Cheshire Branch of the Territorial Army. Like his father he also became chairman of the board of governors of Stockport Grammar School, and again like his father, he was chairman of Swain & Co. (the proprietors of the Advertiser Group of Newspapers). Another chairmanship was that of Stockport's Magistrates Bench that he held for seven years. In 1974, immediately after his retirement from the bench, he was appointed High Sheriff of Cheshire. During the 1970's he was a director of Associated British Hat Manufacturers Ltd.

In 1980 the name of the hatting firm reverted back to Christy & Co.Ltd after A.B.H.M. had sold off its subsidiary (Christy & Co.) to the London property company of Cadogan Estates. The Hillgate site then became the last remaining factory in the Stockport area for hat manufacture. Canal Street and South Mill were sold off reducing the site to 6 acres. In 1996 Christys' employed 190 people when they were taken over by the Priory Company. Manufacturing was carried out at Stockport for only another year. Christy & Co. finally closed in December 1997. Some employees were transferred to Tottington near Bury where only the finishing side of the business was continued with the assistance of six skilled hatters. The Stockport firm that had once been the largest hat manufacturer in Europe and famous for making Winston Churchill's top hats and Geoffrey Boycott's panamas was no longer. Except for No.27 Higher Hillgate the site was cleared in 1999 in preparation for the building of residential and office buildings. Appropriately the proposed premises will be called *Hatters Court* and will comprise three main blocks with the nostalgic names of *Fedora* House , *Homburg* House, and *Bowler* House.

Information Sources:- *Christys' Hat Works* by Penny McKnight
Stockport Advertiser (November and December 1965)

Churchgate Mill

O.S.ref. SJ899 903

Some of the earliest of Stockport's industrial activities started around Churchgate and the neighbouring Carrs. The transition from silk to cotton appears to have started in this area, the Churchgate Mill site on Lavenders Brow being one example where this is thought to have happened. *The Stockport Advertiser* of 14th May 1830 carried an advertisement for the sale of a silk spinning mill at Churchgate mentioning 'cording, spinning, dressing, and double machinery and a quantity of waste silk.' However Churchgate Mill was allegedly built for Peter Marsland in 1828 so was it this mill that was sold in 1830 following Marsland's death the year before? Some years later Churchgate Mill was one of the mills recorded on William Plant's land survey of 1842 '*Plans of all mills etc. in the township of Stockport,*' where the owners were quoted as Elkanah and Samuel H. Cheetham. These plans indicated that parts of the mill were set up for spindle making and bobbin turning. Previously Elkanah Cheetham's name was listed in the 1837 Directory for Stockport as a Cotton Doubler at Fogg Brook.

After the Cheetham's occupation (about 1890), Isaac Pearson & Co. took over and remained there at least until 1907, but by 1910 Pearsons were known only to have operated from Goyt Mills on Newbridge Lane. They were a member company of The Fine Spinners and Doublers Association. The firm of W.H.Mellor Ltd. then moved in around 1925, trading as 'cotton wadding, felt, flock and millpuff manufacturers,' and continued their operation at least until 1954. It was during their occupation of the mill that it is believed the boilers and square sectioned chimney were last in use, steam engines of unknown make being utilised. In 1968 the mill was still owned by the Mellor family, but let off in sections for businesses as diverse as sheet metal spinning, toffee making and domestic appliances, the latter (Peter Cook) eventually taking over the premises.

Information Sources:- *Stockport History Trail* by Stockport Education Authority
Arthur Pike of Crescent Metal Spinning Co.
Stockport Trade Directories

Coronation Mills

O.S.ref. SJ893 916

In the days of the Ashton Canal

The heading for this article is in the plural because there were two mills on this site – namely Coronation Mill and Bankside Mill. Originally set up for cotton spinning in the 1830's, both mills were occupied by Joseph and Thomas Read. The firm of J & T Read was recorded in the Stockport Trade Directory for 1838 as 'cotton spinners and manufacturers by power.' Joseph and Thomas had previously been cotton spinners in Portwood from 1821. Depending on which directory one referred, J & T Read were recorded in one or other of the two mills each year up until 1874. The next recorded occupier of Coronation Mill was the firm of Balfe & Co., 'makers of plain gassed and knotless doubled yarns,' with George Balfe, the principal, residing at *Coronation House* between 1887 and 1893. Also at that time (1893) another firm of cotton doublers – Thomas Rivett Ltd, occupied Bankside Mill. The firm of Rivett (later Joseph Rivett) remained at Bankside until 1936 when the Manchester firm of British Metal Crates took over the premises. It was this latter firm that last used the chimney for exhausting the fumes from their galvanising plant. Galvanising was used to protect the steel strip used by B.M.C. in the construction of crates for carrying milk bottles, beer bottles, and later for carrying silk spools. It must have been necessary for British Metal Crates to increase the draught on the chimney as the original octagonal section brick chimney had been raised in height by about 10 ft. by adding a steel tube at the top. The chimney was lowered and capped off around 1997. British Metal Crates closed in 1976 and thereafter Bankside Mill was no longer referred to, as the owners of neighbouring Coronation Mill took over the premises.

After the occupation by George Balfe, Coronation Mill underwent another change of ownership in 1899 to John Whittaker & Co. who took over as cotton doublers and remained there until 1935. In that year British Trimmings moved into Coronation Mill in order to expand their business which was previously confined to two floors within the Calico Printers Association Mill at Compstall. British Trimmings was set up by Alfred Challinor Stone on1[st] April 1929 from his headquarters at the *Norfolk Arms*, Marple Bridge.

At Coronation Mill Mr.Stone's business of making fringes, pipings, curtain tape and lace developed successfully and included a good export market to Australia, New Zealand and South Africa. One machine was reported to be producing braid for doll's prams at the rate of 400 metres per hour. During the 1950's the trade name of "Britril" was introduced. In 1965 British Trimmings acquired Harris Trimmings of London and three years later purchased a firm in Leek, Staffordshire, that became British Trimmings (Leek) Ltd. which the company used to produce 75% of their dyeing. In 1972 they became part of the Rexmore Group. Also in that year two old established firms in Macclesfield joined them so that the concern became the largest manufacturer of trimmings in the U.K. The business was further enhanced in 1974 by the acquisition of Narrow Fabrics Ltd. of Barrow. A double celebration occurred in 1979. Firstly it was the year of the company's golden jubilee and secondly a £1.5 M extension was opened. To perform the opening ceremony they appropriately engaged Bill Roche (star of TV's *Coronation Street*) to cut the tape.

A takeover by the Beresford Group of Congleton occurred in 1983 after the existing firm had been hit by foreign imports and a changing market. Sensitive to the need for change the company set about the development of a new range of trimmings using prettier, lighter fabrics which they marketed under the new trademark *Spectrum*, quickly establishing their products with the big high street retailers. A new line was set up in the factory to produce ladies garments and theatrical costumes with sequins. Also another section was started for weaving carbon fibre into army belts and parachute harnesses under contract to the Ministry of Defence. By 1997 the workforce had peaked to around 400 people but after yet another takeover, this time by the American Conso Group, some of the production lines were sold off with a resultant reduction in employees to around 240. British Trimmings Ltd. entered the 21st century concentrating on the production of furniture trimmings which include lampshade fringes, curtain tie-backs, and upholstery edgings.

BRITISH TRIMMINGS
===LIMITED===

Manufacturers of
FRINGES, RUCHES, PIPINGS,
COACH LACE,
DRESS TRIMMINGS

CORONATION MILLS
STOCKPORT

STOCKPORT   AND   MONARCH
2 0 3 5   LONDON   5 1 3 4

Advert from the *Stockport Official Handbook* of 1953

Information Sources:-
Newspaper cuttings – Stockport L.H.Library
Bernard Dewhurst – British Trimmings Ltd.

Davies & Metcalfe plc
O.S.ref. SJ938 907

Allegedly this company started as iron bedstead manufacturers, but the partnership between David Davies and James Metcalfe really began in 1879 when they set up to produce steam injectors for boilers. Working under the auspices of the Patent Exhaust Steam Injector Co. of St Anne's Square, Manchester they developed and produced the Davies, Metcalfe, and Hamer patent 'Exhaust' Injector, thus winning the highest award at the 1885 London Inventions Exhibition. This invention was based on the venturi principal, the first injector being patented by Henri Giffard in 1858, but James Metcalfe was responsible for the automatic injector that enabled water in a boiler to be replenished while under pressure and over a wide temperature range. This was especially applied to steam railway locomotives and the firm of Davies & Metcalfe grew as a result. Other products were developed based on the same principle, including high pressure jet cleaning equipment and vacuum brake equipment for railway rolling stock. In order to test their own products D & M required a supply of steam. They generated this from two Babcock & Wilcox water tube boilers installed around 1930. The square sectioned chimney attached to the boiler house was about 80ft. tall, but there was another chimney, taken down in the 1930's that previously served the foundry. As the boilers had excess capacity they were also used via heat exchangers to heat parts of the factory. Over the years the premises housed a variety of power generators. There were two horizontal steam engines in the early 1900's. One of them called *Gwendoline* was used to generate electricity at 110 volts which was common up to about 1930. There was also a gas engine at one time but all of these were replaced by electric motors in the 1930's.

The company had a long association with railways, and over the years five generations of Metcalfe's were involved with the firm which employed some 500 people in the 1970's. The company was taken over in 1992 by the German firm of Thyssen that in turn became part of the SABWABCO Group in 1996. They subsequently closed the Romiley site in favour of a smaller plant in Hyde. Sadly this

too was facing closure at the time of writing, but Richard Metcalfe (junior) has kept injector overhaul and manufacture alive by forming the new firm of Metcalfe Railway Products Ltd.

Information Sources:- *A Short History of Bredbury & Romiley* by Robert Hunter
Article in *Old Glory* magazine February 1999
Richard Metcalfe (senior)

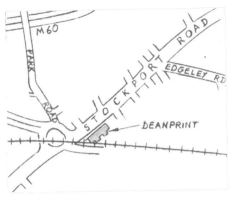

Deanprint Ltd.
O.S.ref.SJ869 891

The construction of the print works at Cheadle Heath in 1920 was the culmination of hard work in the career of its founder – Joseph Dean. Deanprint Ltd. as the company is known today, owes its existence to the determination of Joseph Dean whose interesting working life started in a woollen mill in Yorkshire in 1855, being then only seven years old. Whilst there he applied his alertness and clear thinking to improving the mill machinery by making adjustments that increased productivity. This was brought to the attention of the representative of the machinery manufacturers and as a result Joseph was offered the job of overseeing the installation and commissioning of that company's machinery in France. The year was 1870 and prior to leaving for France he married Elizabeth Bottomley in Halifax. After three years in France he was back in England looking for another job and was fortunate to acquire the position of foreman in the wool forming department of a hat factory. This was his introduction to Stockport for the hat factory was Christy's. During his employment at Christys' he used his knowledge of French to organise a trip to Paris for some of the hatters. Resulting from this the Manchester, Sheffield, and Lincolnshire Railway approached Joseph Dean with a proposition to set up an agency. This he did and as a consequence he opened his first office in the Borough Chambers, High Street, Stockport. Consecutively a number of partners linked with Joseph Dean, but it was a Mr.Dawson who finally teamed up with Joseph to form the travel agency of Dean & Dawson. As this business progressed it became apparent that they were being repeatedly let down by their printers, especially the printing of handbills and posters on time. In order to rectify this situation they purchased their own printing machine and from this emerged the beginning of Deanprint. The travel agency of Dean & Dawson flourished with offices opening in most major towns and by the 1920's they were advertising tours and cruises to all parts of the world. Eventually this side of the Dean family business was integrated into the Thomas Cook Travel Co.

Whilst the printing business progressed, Joseph Dean struck up a friendship with Giles Atherton, a prominent member of the hatting industry and twice Mayor of Stockport. This led to Dean & Co.(Stockport) Ltd. operating as manufacturers of hats and speciality leathers from premises known as Royal Oak Works. By the 1910's Dean & Co. were operating from three separate factories and decided to look for more suitable premises. Hence the building of Cheadle Heath Works. It was the intention to call the new premises *Royal Oak Works* but as doubt was raised as to the legality of using the word "royal" the title was dropped. However not to be completely severed from the past, two oak trees were planted at the front of the site to mark the occasion of the commencement of building. These trees are still thriving. Early photographs show the factory chimney with a crown, but the chimney today is straight sided and 80ft. tall. It was built quite ornately on a square plinth with corbelled coping and some cleverly designed corner stones to merge the square of the plinth to an octagonal section chimney. Little is known of the use of the chimney but it is more likely to have served the tannery rather than the printing side of the business. Leather processing was phased out by the 1950's leaving the company to concentrate on printing and bookbinding which it does today. The workforce peaked to 220 in the 1960's.

Joseph Dean and Elizabeth Bottomley were married for over 60 years and lived to see their son Joseph Normanton Dean become chairman of the company in 1928. Joseph Dean was appointed Justice of the Peace in 1914 and represented the old Edgeley Ward on the Stockport Town Council. He was also made an Alderman of the Borough. In addition to his business interests outlined above he was one of the founders of the Ring Spinning Mills, and for a brief period was associated with T.W.Bracher & Co., another supplier of hat leathers. Both Dean & Co. and T.W.Bracher & Co. went their separate ways following a dispute but both companies have survived, the latter still trading in hat leathers. In 1958 Alan Dean, grandson of the founder, succeeded Joseph Normanton as Chairman of the company, the third generation to take that position. Since then the company has progressed taking new technology in its stride. In 1990 the company celebrated 100 years and to mark that occasion they published their own centenary book entitled Yesteryears- A History of Deanprint Ltd.

Corner stones that convert the square plinth to the octagonal chimney

Information Source:- Michael Marren of Deanprint Ltd.

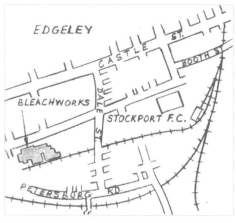
Situation in 1960 when branch railway line served the bleachworks

Edgeley Bleachworks
O.S.ref. SJ885 890

Edgeley Bleachworks was an alternative name for Sykes & Co. Ltd. (bleachers and finishers) who were amongst the best known manufacturing companies in Stockport. The business was established in 1793 by William Sykes, a Yorkshireman from Wakefield. Initially his business consisted of bleaching cloth supplied to him by local handloom weavers, and then purveying it to various linen drapers. As in the case of many industrial concerns the site was selected for its access to water, a stream running right through the shallow valley on which the works was built. Water power was originally used, but the works saw its first steam engine as early as 1803. Over the years many more powerful engines were installed or replaced so that by 1910 there were 29 stationary steam engines entered in the inventory carried out by the firm of valuers and assessors engaged for insurance purposes. To the observer the use of 29 engines at any one time would seem to be an inefficient way of working, but the bleachworks was not built like a multi-storey cotton mill with a single power source. Instead Sykes' comprised of many single storey sheds housing a range of different processes.

Around the 1850's the reservoirs, that have today become a recreational attraction, were constructed. This happened following the recommendation of John Dalton, the famous chemist, whom Sykes & Co. engaged as consultant on the quality of their water supply. Water supplied from reservoirs was reckoned to partially alleviate the problems of scale build-up in the boilers. In 1910 there were six Lancashire boilers on site supplied by William Lord of Bury. So many boilers indicate a large steam installation necessitating a big chimney and Sykes' chimney at 302ft. was alleged to have been the tallest in Stockport.

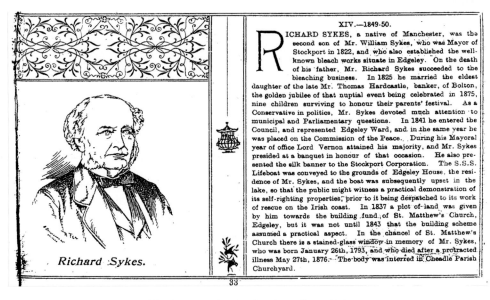

From *Mayors of Stockport 1836 – 96* : Stockport Central Library

In addition to the visible landmark of a tall chimney, Sykes' were remembered by the local residents for the audible factory hooter. Not only did it summon employees to attend work but was alleged to have sounded off at 10 o'clock in the evening as a signal to the manager at home that everything was in order at the factory. Parents in the vicinity welcomed this sound to check if their teenage children had come home off the streets.

On the death of William, his son Richard Sykes took control of the company, guiding the firm through many technical developments. Richard Sykes did much for the community and like his father became Mayor of Stockport. The Sykes family created a unique record in the history of the Borough of Stockport in that four generations of Sykes held the office of Mayor: William in 1822, Richard in 1849, Arthur Henry in 1880, and Colonel Sir Alan Sykes in 1910. They also had active roles in the governing of Stockport Infirmary as did Captain Thomas Hardcastle Sykes (grandson of the founder) who was a committee member from 1864 and later Honorary Treasurer until his death in1901.

In 1900 Sykes & Co. became part of the Bleachers Association with Sir Alan Sykes as its chairman. The Edgeley works specialised in processing fully shrunk materials and washable fire-repellant finishes. In 1966 they were employing 180 people and processing more than 200 miles of material per week. Huge quantities of water was necessary, and Sykes' were fortunate in having artesian wells in addition to their storage reserves. Even in times of drought the wells were never known to have failed. One in particular was termed *The Silver Well* by Richard Sykes on account of the sparkle of the water. The steam driven pumping engine for this well was still in place when the factory closed, although it had not run for years, and possibly qualifies as the longest surviving stationary steam engine in Stockport. There were good intentions to restore and preserve this engine and to this end it was transported in a stripped down condition to the Steamtown Museum, Carnforth. However no further action was taken and when the author made a visit to the museum many parts were found to be missing. In an attempt to preserve something from Sykes's past he has made a working model of this engine based on photographs from Stockport Library archives, and with measurements of the engine relics at Carnforth.

Edgeley Bleachworks closed in 1986 and therefore strictly missed the target of survival into the 1990's that this book covers. However for a company that meant so much to Stockport and its people, and a family of directors that played such important roles in the community, it surely deserves a mention. The site was cleared and three attractive housing estates were built in its place, the artesian well water having been taken care of in underground culverts. Today, all that physically remains of this once influential company are the reservoirs.

SYKES & CO., LTD.

BLEACHERS AND FINISHERS

ESTABLISHED 1793

PROCESSING

Polymark laundry-marking cloths; apron cloths; cotton and nylon typewriter cloths. Trubenised collar linings; thermoplastic and heat-setting resin finishes on cotton and rayon interlinings; Bleacraft "Sanforised" and "Staffix" fully-shrunk finishes; insulation cloth finishes on straight or bias materials; open width scouring and bleaching of wigans and heavy industrial fabrics; coated finishes for fusible interlinings; FLAME RETARDENT FINISHING OF FURNISHINGS AND INDUSTRIAL CLOTHS

ALL INDUSTRIAL ENQUIRIES WELCOMED AT

EDGELEY BLEACHWORKS STOCKPORT

Telephone: 061-480 4807/8/9.

84

From the *Stockport Official Handbook* for 1976

Information Sources :-
    The Romance of Industry – Stockport Advertiser, 31st March 1922
    William Sykes & The Edgeley Bleachworks 1755-1837 by Phyllis M Giles M.A.
    Sykes Inventory of 31st March 1910 – Quarry Bank Mill Archives

Hallam Mill

O.S. ref. SJ900 887

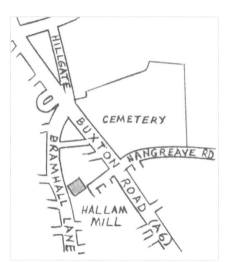

From details extracted from the records it is difficult to be certain when Hallam Mill dates from, for one report states that *Heaviley Mill* (as it was also called) was built for Ephraim Hallam in 1859. However it had already been featured in the survey of 1842 carried out by William Plant (land surveyor) entitled *Plans of all Mills, etc. in the township of Stockport*, where it shows the mill belonging to Ephraim Hallam complete with the separate chimney close to *Hallam Passage* as it exists today. To add to the confusion the Stockport Trade Directory for 1845 lists Ephraim Hallam as a cotton spinner of Hillgate mills, Higher Hillgate. Whatever the origin, we do know that Hallam Mill was used for cotton waste spinning, and was built to a greater width than earlier mills to accommodate longer mules. The octagonal section chimney, typical of 19th century construction, now stands about 110ft. high but was once much taller with a top crown. Steam was certainly raised to power engines but nothing is known of their particulars. By 1897 the mill ran 31,000 spindles. Mill owner Ephraim Hallam involved himself in community affairs, became a councillor in 1844, and rose to become Mayor of Stockport in 1862, the year of the great cotton famine. His endeavours in maintaining the morale of the townsfolk during that period of hardship were widely praised. He died on Christmas Day 1897 age 89, and not long after cotton spinning at the mill ceased.

By 1905 Squirrel Confectionery had moved in and remained there for the next 60 years becoming especially famous for their *Dolly Mixture* sweets. The words 'SQUIRREL CONFECTIONERY WORKS' were marked on the brickwork of the wall of the main mill building that over looks the A6 London Road but are barely visible today. In July 1964, after many years of competition with their neighbours on the other side of the A6, Squirrel merged with John Horn Ltd. to become Squirrel Horn. They closed the Hallam Street works in 1968 but continued in business in Canada Street, struggling against repeated arson attacks until finally moving to Glenrothes under Alma Holdings in October 1990. Following the withdrawal of Squirrel Confectionery from Hallam Mill in 1968, Hallam Associates were formed about 1971, letting off sections of the mill for various industrial uses. This situation has continued through to the present time except that the premises are now managed by different landlords. Activities include a mailing service company, shirt manufacture and paint manufacture, the twenty or so firms employing up to 200 people between them.

XXIII—1862-3.

EPHRAIM HALLAM was apprenticed to a chemist and apothecary, whose business premises were in Underbank. The youth studied Latin and attended the chemistry lectures of Professor Davies (assistant to Dr. John Dalton), Manchester. Mr. Hallam then commenced business on his own behalf as a chemist and druggist, afterwards turning his attention to cotton-waste spinning. Success waited upon him, and finally the Heaviley Mill was established. He became a town councillor in 1844, was elevated to the aldermanic bench in 1858, elected Mayor in 1862, placed on the Commission of the Peace for the borough during the following year, and was appointed a county magistrate in 1884. For many years he has been regarded as "the Father of the Council" and the oldest magistrate in the borough. During his Chief Magistracy the Prince of Wales was married, an address signed by Alderman Hallam, on behalf of the borough, being forwarded to his Royal Highness and the Princess of Wales. Mr. Hallam has identified himself with the interests of many local institutions, and exercised his energetic capabilities and generosity during the period of widespread distress and gloom which prevailed in the town. He is intimately associated with the local history of the Methodist New Connexion, and was the representative of the Stockport Circuit between the years 1858-79. Born on March 11th, 1812, Alderman Hallam, despite his venerable age, is occasionally seen on the magisterial bench, and also attends, as an alderman, meetings of the Council. His residence is Oakwood Hall, Romiley.

Ephraim Hallam.

Hallam Passage

A 90 hour week ?

Information Sources :-
Newspaper cuttings – Stockport Central Library
Stockport : A History – P.Arrowsmith

Heaton Mersey Bleachworks

O.S. ref.SJ867 901

One of the many initiatives started by Samuel Oldknow was the establishment in 1785 of a bleaching, dyeing and printing business at Heaton Mersey. It was situated at the bottom of Vale Road on the north bank of the River Mersey, ideally placed for the supply of water for which it was heavily dependant. By 1791 when Samuel's brother Thomas was the managing partner, the business employed 37 printers. In spite of Samuel Oldknow's ultimate success he nevertheless came across hard times and, following a business downturn in 1792 and 1793 was, forced to jettison his works at both Heaton Mersey and Anderton, concentrating production at Mellor Mill for which he became well known.

Ownership fell into the hands of Robert Parker who ran both this (the Lower Bleachworks) and Upper Bleachworks, situated higher up Vale Road. Best remembered for his benevolence within the district, Robert Parker saw the need for a proper place of worship and in 1805 founded the Sunday School at Heaton Mersey, where both education and religious instruction were taught, there being no day schools in the vicinity at the time. Robert Parker died in 1815 as the result of a tragic road accident.

Samuel Stocks became the next owner, and ran the business from about 1824 until some time in the 1840's when he became bankrupt. The tithe map for Heaton Mersey dated 1848 indicated that the fields on each side of Vale Road belonged to George Young, and it was George Young & Co. who occupied the bleachworks in 1851. During the 1850's there were further changes of occupancy, one being Mortimer Laviter Tait, who had a block of houses built near the top of Vale Road for housing apprentices, the house bricks being obtained from a demolished chimney at the works. In the 1860's Frank Melland and E. Coward, two Manchester businessmen, established the firm of Melland & Coward that was to survive for a further 130 years. Messrs Melland & Coward were known to have possessed their own fire engine, but in 1871 they still found it necessary to call out Stockport Fire Brigade's first steam fire engine – a Merryweather - to a fire at the works. Described in the early years as *bleachers, cotton spinners and manufacturers,* Melland & Coward had 23,300 spindles and 430 looms by 1897. A weir on the River Mersey provided a head of water to drive a water wheel, and to supply one reservoir and three filter beds. A cut through the premises returned the water to the river about ¼ mile downstream. In the 1920's some of the more substantial boilers were fuelled by coal and the octagonal sectioned chimney was built. At 232ft high it became, in 1986, the tallest chimney remaining in Stockport. Melland & Coward's production was mainly based on the output of the coarser grade cloths for such uses as book covers, bag cloths and abrasives such as emery cloth. Like so many bleachers, they became members of the Bleaching Association in 1900, but continued to trade under the name of Melland & Coward Ltd. up until their closure in September 1992, by which time they were a subsidiary of Whitecroft plc. There were 82 employees at Heaton Mersey when the bleachworks closed and some were offered jobs by Whitecroft at another of their plants in Bolton. Finally the site was cleared, the magnificent chimney coming down in 1995. The site was then advertised for redevelopment of industrial units under the heading of *Kings Park.*

Poignant reflection in one of the filter beds

Advert from the 1953 edition of the *Stockport Official Handbook*

There were a lot of bricks used in a chimney with these proportions

Information Sources:- *Samuel Oldknow* by Tom Oldham
Heaton Mersey, A Victorian Village by Joe Eaton

Hempshaw Brook Brewery

O.S.ref. SJ903 895

Brewing was established on this site as far back as 1836 by Avery Fletcher who advertised the sale of Ale and Porter, the quality of which he claimed was due to the purity of the water from the Hempshaw Brook. By 1851 Avery Fletcher had withdrawn from this business and Joseph Smith and Henry Bell took control, trading as *Smith and Bell*. This partnership flourished for 20 years, Joseph Smith retiring in 1872 leaving Henry Bell as chairman of the new firm – *Bell & Co*. Henry Bell was yet another industrialist to become Mayor of Stockport, in Bell's case for two terms. The business grew from strength to strength with Henry Bell Junior taking over after his father's death in 1891. The brewery became a limited company in 1897. Henry Bell Junior followed the same pattern as his father, becoming Mayor of Stockport and also like his father, served in that capacity for two terms – 1906/7. Trade at the brewery was seriously depleted during the Great War but by 1926 they were confident enough to plan a new building on the same site. This opened in 1930 and is the building we see today. During the construction the builders took the opportunity to advertise the company by incorporating the words 'BELL & Co LIMITED HEMPSHAW BROOK BREWERY' into the brickwork above the second floor. This can just be discerned from Hempshaw Lane if one looks carefully. In 1949 Frederick Robinson's brewery took over and continued to use the premises for some years.

Today *European Colour (Pigments) Ltd.* occupy the premises. They were originally in Bankfield Street at the top of Lancashire Hill, but moved to the Hempshaw Lane site in 1978 where they were able to benefit from two particular features, one being the presence of an artesian well. The other advantage was having a multi-storey building, thus allowing the processes to be arranged from the top down using gravity to propel the work in progress. Steam, necessary for their manufacturing process, was produce by means of a gas fired boiler, but over the years the accompanying chimney exhausted fumes from solid fuel, oil and gas firings. The round section chimney in the photographs was a very slender one standing at about 125ft. and was one of the few in use in Stockport up to the year 2001 when it was replaced by a modern steel equivalent.

European Colour have established themselves as market leaders in the production of organic pigments which are aimed primarily at the printing inks market, especially those used in the consumer packaging sector.

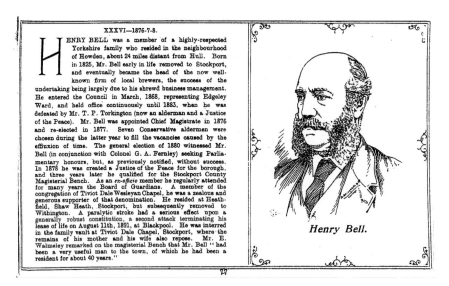

XXXVI—1876-7-8.

HENRY BELL was a member of a highly-respected Yorkshire family who resided in the neighbourhood of Howden, about 24 miles distant from Hull. Born in 1825, Mr. Bell early in life removed to Stockport, and eventually became the head of the now well-known firm of local brewers, the success of the undertaking being largely due to his shrewd business management. He entered the Council in March, 1868, representing Edgeley Ward, and held office continuously until 1883, when he was defeated by Mr. T. P. Torkington (now an alderman and a Justice of the Peace). Mr. Bell was appointed Chief Magistrate in 1876 and re-elected in 1877. Seven Conservative aldermen were chosen during the latter year to fill the vacancies caused by the effluxion of time. The general election of 1880 witnessed Mr. Bell (in conjunction with Colonel G. A. Fernley) seeking Parliamentary honours, but, as previously notified, without success. In 1878 he was created a Justice of the Peace for the borough, and three years later he qualified for the Stockport County Magisterial Bench. As an *ex-officio* member he regularly attended for many years the Board of Guardians. A member of the congregation of Tiviot Dale Wesleyan Chapel, he was a zealous and generous supporter of that denomination. He resided at Heathfield, Shaw Heath, Stockport, but subsequently removed to Withington. A paralytic stroke had a serious effect upon a generally robust constitution, a second attack terminating his lease of life on August 11th, 1891, at Blackpool. He was interred in the family vault at Tiviot Dale Chapel, Stockport, where the remains of his mother and his wife also repose. Mr. E. Walmsley remarked on the magisterial Bench that Mr. Bell "had been a very useful man to the town, of which he had been a resident for about 40 years."

Henry Bell.

From *Mayors of Stockport 1836-96* :Stockport Central Library

Information Sources:- *A History of Stockport Breweries* – Mike Ogden
Stuart Foster of European Colour (Pigments) Ltd.

Hope Mill

O.S.ref.SJ897 910

Like so many mills, this one was built close to the riverbank, and there is some evidence that it was in existence in the 1790's, although probably not the same buildings as those seen 200 years later. However more reliable evidence in the form of an early map indicated that the oldest buildings dated back to 1817 and there was also a date on the chimney - 1838. The premises were known as *Higher and Lower Hope Mills* and built on the south bank of the River Tame for cotton spinning. By the mid 19th century the buildings also included a gas works (not unusual in those days), which was for the exclusive use of the owners. The chimney was more unusual in that it was built with a high degree of batter such that it resembled an obelisk rather than the usual factory chimney. The earliest known owner/occupier was Thomas Wheildon, a cotton heald yarn manufacturer, whose residence was given as Queen Street for 1837 and 1841, but operating industrially in Pool Lane, in the latter year. The first positive mention of *Hope Mill* was for 1845 when two cotton spinners were listed in the Stockport Directory for that year. One was Thomas Wheildon, living then in New Zealand Road, and the other – John Cooper of Preston. They were still there in 1857 but by 1864 all trace of them had disappeared

Thomas and James Leigh, who had entered into partnership in 1850 and already owned *Beehive Mill*, took over Hope Mills in 1871. Messrs. T & J Leigh were operational as cotton spinners at Hope Mill until 1942 but later concentrated their production at both *Beehive* and *Meadow Mill* that they also owned. Manufacturing changed radically at *Hope Mill* in 1942 to rubber sheet production under the name of *Celoform Ltd*. Celoform had previously been in business in Harriet Street manufacturing sponge rubber. They remained at *Hope Mill* for the next 20 years and were sometimes listed in the trade directories as Celford (Stockport) Ltd. Their principal product was rubber sheeting for the footware industry. The name changed to the *Sam Kay Rubber Co. Ltd.* around 1962/3 and

Hope Mill in 1994 showing the Alligator factory in the background –
both since demolished

then in about 1971 the firm merged with a French company called Salpa to become *Salpa Kay Ltd.* By 1981 this firm became part of the Chamberlain Phipps Group and they were producing some 40,000 one metre square sheets of rubber per week for shoe soles, employing a workforce of 30 people. A similar factory to Salpa Kay was operated by Chamberlain Phipps in Yeovil, Somerset where costs were lower due to it being purpose built. Consequently when sales dwindled the company decided to close down the Stockport operation. This took place in January 1996 but it was not the last time that Hope Mill was to feature in the newspapers.

After being derelict for over two years the mill suddenly burst into flames one Saturday in October 1998 giving rise to a front page headline in the Stockport Express – "Town Centre grinds to halt as mill burns." Probably started by pranksters the blaze was spectacular sending flames 100ft. into the air. Ten fire engines were called to the scene. Thick black smoke from the burning tar pitch roof

caused motorway traffic to slow down to watch, but fortunately there were no human casualties. Nearly half of the buildings collapsed into the River Tame. A few weeks later the whole site was cleared leaving no trace of Hope Mill after its 180 years of activity.

A 1949 Advert

A view up the River Tame – Meadow Mill in the distance

Information Sources:- *Stockport Official Handbook* (for 1949 and 1953)
Stockport Messenger for 19th October 1995
Stockport Express for 7th October 1998

The Ashton Canal still present in the 1960.s

Houldsworth Mill
Reddish
O.S.ref. SJ891 933

The cotton spinning firm first established by Thomas Houldsworth in the 1790's was once the sixth largest in the town of Manchester. In 1865, following it's early success and scale of business, led the founder's nephew, William Henry Houldsworth, to build a new five storey mill at Reddish alongside the Ashton Canal. He engaged the architect A.H.Stott of Oldham, who designed a 'double mill' – i.e. two main blocks for spinning symmetrically placed each side of a central block used for main entrance, offices and warehousing. He flanked the central block each side with a stair tower capped with pyramid shaped roofs. In addition he set a clock on the parapet and generally lavished a high level of architectural features in the *Italianate Style* to distinguish his mill. Consistent with the front façade, the rear of the mill was built with equal symmetry, having a centrally placed engine house and chimney exactly on the centre line. The octagonal section chimney was given as much architectural embellishment as the

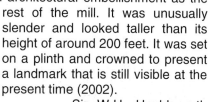

rest of the mill. It was unusually slender and looked taller than its height of around 200 feet. It was set on a plinth and crowned to present a landmark that is still visible at the present time (2002).

Sir W.H. Houldsworth provided more for Reddish than just his mill, building terraced housing for the workers and a working men's club designed also by A.H. Stott. He also engaged another architect, Alfred Waterhouse R.A. (designer of Manchester Town Hall) to design the school for the community, the rectory, and the church of St.Elizabeth.

In 1898 the mill became part of the Fine Cotton Spinners and Doublers Association. Two years later the firm decided to replace the original upright drive shafts with rope drives. This was an opportune time to replace the engines as well. New engine houses were required for this and as a result the rule of symmetry regarding the building plan was upset to a degree. A vertical cross compound steam engine made by J & E Wood was installed in the engine house for the south block and a vertical side by side compound steam engine made by Scott & Hodgson was installed in the north engine house. The boilers were manufactured by Thomas Beeley. By 1920 Fine Cotton Spinners and Doublers were running 140,000 spindles at Reddish and spinning was continued there until 1958.

Following the cessation of spinning at the mill, the building was opened up for various business units. Then in 1999 the suitability of Houldsworth Mill as a project for *Regeneration Through Heritage* was fully realised and transformation began in the conversion of the building into housing association flats, modern business units, a conference centre, and training facilities. Prince Charles visited the mill in 1997 in his role as president of *Regeneration Through Heritage*. This fine looking building is Grade II* listed and had £9 million spent on it, contributed by a consortium composed of Stockport Council, the Heaton and Houldsworth Property Company, Northern Counties Housing Association, English Partnerships, and the European Regional Development Fund.

Information Sources:-
   Cotton Mills in Greater Manchester by M.Williams & D.A.Farnie
   Houldsworth Cotton Mill by Patricia Hayes (Stockport Central Library)

McVitie's Bakery

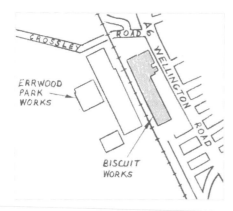

Crossley Road O.S.ref. SJ878 931

The story of McVitie's starts not surprisingly in Scotland in 1830, when Robert McVitie (an apprentice baker from Dumfries) started a bakery in the basement of a tenement building in Rose Street, Edinburgh. By the middle of the 19th century he had established a high quality retail bakery and confectionery business. In 1888 Robert teamed up with Charles Price who was an expert in selling, and so the company of *McVitie & Price* was formed. Charles stayed with the firm for 13 years, leaving in 1901 when he became a Liberal M.P. By then the company was well recognised and so the name *McVitie & Price* was retained in spite of Charles Price's absence. Robert McVitie died in 1884 and was succeeded by his son Robert McVitie (junior), who in 1887, astutely engaged Alexander Grant after the latter proved that he could make a better scone than that on offer in the McVitie shop. In 1892 Alexander Grant was responsible for devising the recipe for what was to become the company's most famous biscuit – *The Digestive*. Alexander Grant rose in position in the company to become Chairman and Managing Director after Robert (junior) died. As the business developed , new bakeries were built; first St.Andrew's Biscuit Works in Edinburgh and then in 1901 a new factory in Harlesden, North London, where the Digestive Biscuit was produced in greater quantities than ever before but always to the standard set by Alexander Grant which stipulated the precise diameter of the biscuit as well as it's quality.

As is often the case, the incidence of a major war can bring either tragedy or prosperity to a business. For McVitie & Price the opportunity to expand came during World War 1 when the government of the day requested them to produce "iron ration" plain biscuits. To meet this demand the company decided to open a new bakery and chose a 12 acre site in Stockport for their new factory.

The premises were built by Mark Lane & Co. Ltd. of Heaton Lane, Stockport and opened in 1917 on the Heaton Chapel - Levenshulme border. Consequently because of this location both Stockport and Manchester include McVitie's as one of their industrial strengths. Soon after the termination of WW1 the company increased its range of products by spreading chocolate on top of digestive biscuits to create a new popular biscuit – the *Chocolate Homewheat*. Introduced in 1932, *Penguin Biscuits*, made in Stockport, became a great success with sales of over £30 million per year.

Following World War Two, restrictions on supplies and transport led to negotiations being held between McVitie & Price and one of their rival companies – Macfarlane & Lang. The result was the formation, in 1948, of United Biscuits, a title that is still the official company name. However the name *McVitie's* predominates in advertising.

When Value Added Tax came into being, McVitie's ran into trouble with the department of Customs and Excise who wanted to declare McVitie's *Jaffa Cakes* as biscuits thereby being liable for tax. However the company insisted they were cakes and eventually won their case keeping the purchase price down. There were other cakes that contributed to McVitie's fame, all of them Royal Wedding Cakes. The first was in 1893 for the wedding of Princess Mary of Teck to the Duke of York, later to become King George V. The second was in 1923 for the wedding of Elizabeth Bowes-Lyon to the next Duke of York before he became King George VI. Then in 1947 McVitie & Price supplied the cake for the wedding of Prince Philip to Princess Elizabeth (Queen Elizabeth II). In the mid 1980's the Stockport bakery expanded in order to produce *TUC Savoury Crackers*, and in August 1999 another new product line was introduced to produce a chocolate caramel biscuit. The site's permanent borders could unfortunately limit any further expansion of the premises – the A6 Wellington Road to the east and the main Manchester to London railway line to the west.

Early maps of the site indicate the boiler house and chimney were originally sited in the north west corner of the plot near the railway. The present chimney stands nearer the road and is of modern design being parallel sided and built in concrete and stands at 31.2 metres (102ft.) high according to records at the factory. It serves the boilers and to a lesser extent some of the exhaust from the *Combined Heat and Power Units* of which there are two at McVitie's. The first C.H.P. unit was installed in 1992 and the second in 1998. These are energy efficient units fuelled by gas to power turbines that in turn generate up to 1Megawatt of electricity. In the intermediate stages of operation some of the exhaust heat is utilised to generate steam, and some of this can be used to heat the ingredients used in the production of biscuits.

The company has a fine track record on safety, winning awards in 1973 and 1976. In 1992 they were awarded a 5 Star Award by the British Safety Council. Employee numbers have been around the 900 level during the late 1990's maintaining McVitie's as one of the principal employers in the district.

Information Sources:- Stockport Local History Library
McVitie's – *History of McVitie's*
Joanne Mitchell & Frank Johnson of McVitie's

Meadow Mill

Water Street O.S.ref. SJ899 912

Between the River Tame and the
Portwood Cut

The brothers Thomas and James Leigh entered into partnership as cotton spinners in 1850 trading as *T & J Leigh*. However Thomas died in 1857 leaving James as head of the company which, by 1872, owned both *Beehive* and *Hope* mills in the Portwood district of Stockport. With the difficult years of the cotton famine behind it, the firm of T & J Leigh embarked on expansion and so arranged in 1880 for one of the town's first new mills to be built, once again in Portwood and close to the River Tame. The architect for the new building (called Meadow Mill) was George Woodhouse of Bolton, who designed a double mill for the purpose of spinning both cotton and wool. The mill had a basement and six storeys. Noticeable in the centre of each window on the top storey is a cast iron pillar. Cast iron pillars also run along the centre of each floor, with lengthwise and crosswise iron beams supporting brick arches running across the width rather than lengthwise which was traditional up to that time. Being a double mill the engine house was placed centrally, as was the chimney a little further to the west of the main building. As was generally the custom in the late nineteenth century, the chimney was octagonal in section and crowned with a fairly ornamental oversailer. It is about 170ft. tall. Several additions were made to the mill over the years, the one at the south –west corner being most noticeable by the lighter coloured brick raising that part of the building by another two floors. Certainly the original concept was without this addition as shown by an artists impression painted for the architect before building commenced. This painting also illustrated the mill without the two towers, but they are believed to have been there from the beginning. (A reduced size copy of this painting is retained in Stockport Central Library).

In 1910 Messrs. T & J Leigh were described as *cotton, marino, and cashmere spinners* and by 1914 were operating 120.000 spindles. Inevitably World War One depleted the workforce and 22 male employees were not to return. In respect to the fallen, the company mounted a plaque on the mill inscribed: "In memory of the employees of T & J Leigh Ltd. who laid down their lives in the Great War 1914 - 18". This can be seen on the wall outside at the west end of the mill.

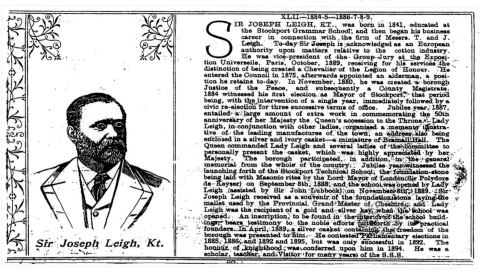

XLII—1884-5—1886-7-8-9.

SIR JOSEPH LEIGH, KT., was born in 1841, educated at the Stockport Grammar School, and then began his business career in connection with the firm of Messrs. T. and J. Leigh. To-day Sir Joseph is acknowledged as an European authority upon matters relative to the cotton industry. He was vice-president of the Group Jury at the Exposition Universelle, Paris, October, 1889, receiving for his services the distinction of being created a Chevalier of the Legion of Honour. He entered the Council in 1875, afterwards appointed an alderman, a position he retains to-day. In November, 1880, he was created a borough Justice of the Peace, and subsequently a County Magistrate. 1884 witnessed his first election as Mayor of Stockport, that period being, with the intervention of a single year, immediately followed by a civic re-election for three successive terms of office. Jubilee year, 1887, entailed a large amount of extra work in commemorating the 50th anniversary of her Majesty the Queen's accession to the Throne. Lady Leigh, in conjunction with other ladies, organised a memento illustrative of the leading manufactures of the town, an address also being enclosed in a silver and ivory casket—a miniature of Bramall Hall. The Queen commanded Lady Leigh and several ladies of the committee to personally present the casket, which was highly appreciated by her Majesty. The borough participated, in addition, in the general memorial from the whole of the country. Jubilee year witnessed the launching forth of the Stockport Technical School, the foundation-stone being laid with Masonic rites by the Lord Mayor of London(Sir Polydore de Keyser) on September 8th, 1888; and the school was opened by Lady Leigh (assisted by Sir John Lubbock) on November 8th, 1889. Sir Joseph Leigh received as a souvenir of the foundationstone laying the mallet used by the Provincial Grand Master of Cheshire; and Lady Leigh was the recipient of a gold and silver key, when the school was opened. An inscription, to be found in the interior of the school buildings, bears testimony to the noble efforts put forth by its practical founders. In April, 1889, a silver casket containing the freedom of the borough was presented to him. He contested Parliamentary elections in 1885, 1886, and 1892 and 1895, but was only successful in 1892. The honour of knighthood was conferred upon him in 1894. He was a scholar, teacher, and Visitor (for many years) of the S.S.S.

Sir Joseph Leigh, Kt.

Apart from directing and managing the firm of T & J Leigh Ltd. several members of the Leigh family became intricately involved in local public affairs and politics. Three of them became Mayor of Stockport, the most notable being Joseph Leigh who was elected to that position four times – in 1884, 1886, 1887 and 1888. His uncle James Leigh was mayor for two terms – 1881 and 1882 - and played a prominent role in the operation of Stockport Sunday School, taking on sole superintendence of the organisation in 1883. Joseph Leigh's other uncle, William, became mayor in 1885 and he also was closely associated with Stockport Sunday School, being honorary secretary and sub-treasurer at the time of his death. Joseph had a most distinguished career, culminating with a knighthood in 1894. He was the grandson of the founder cotton spinner – Thomas Leigh.

T. & J. LEIGH LTD.

Cotton and Worsted Spinners

MEADOW MILLS, STOCKPORT

AERIAL VIEW OF MEADOW MILLS

AN OLD-ESTABLISHED FIRM with up-to-date ideas, it provides excellent working conditions for its workers. A modern nursery looks after the young children of women employees whilst at work and a fully qualified nurse with well-fitted first-aid and rest rooms gives treatment when necessary to all employees.

A good canteen, 2 bowling greens, 2 billiards ta les and well laid out gardens afford recreation at lunchtime and after working hours.

PRODUCTS. The Company is noted in the trade for its high quality Yarns. We are spinners of Hosiery, Coloured Mixture Yarns, Wool and Cotton Mixtures, Grandrelles and Mock Grandrelles and various synthetic mixtures. Counts 4 to 40. Also makers of " Meadowool " Hand Knitting Wools.

Advert from the 1953 edition of the Stockport Official Handbook

He married the eldest daughter of Sir Daniel Adamson (of Manchester Ship Canal fame) and became Member of Parliament for Stockport for two terms, 1892 –5, and 1900 –6. He was instrumental in promoting the limited companies that led to the construction of Vernon and Palmer Mills. Sir Joseph died in September 1908 age 67 years. A bust of Sir Joseph is on display in Stockport Town Hall.

T & J Leigh Ltd. continued spinning until the Cotton Re-organisation Act came into being in the 1950's. The scheme was to 'scrap all spindles and carding engines in their cotton and carpet yarn spinning branches.' Under this scheme T & J Leigh received £65,538 from The Cotton Board for scrapped machinery. Overall the government scheme was a streamlining plan valued at £30 Million nationally. Employees at Meadow Mill (of which there were about 300 women and 100 men in the cotton section) were warned of the possible closure in August 1959 and subsequently T & J Leigh Ltd. shut down on 31st March 1960. A syndicate called Hursbaris Investments Ltd. then took over and a new company was formed called *Leigh's (Stockport) Ltd.* that carried on spinning worsted and carpet yarn until 1969. Ever since then the mill has been owned by various estate managers and let out to a variety of industrial users. At one time as many as 44 companies were listed. Amongst them are furniture upholsterers, metal spinners, printers, and glaziers.

Information Sources:-
Industrial Archaeology of Stockport by Owen Ashmore
Mayors of Stockport 1836-96: Stockport Central Library
Stockport Cen.Lib: folders on *Sir Joseph Leigh* and *Meadow Mill*
David Taylor of Elegant Upholstery
Brigadier C. Bromby (Sir Joseph Leigh's Grandson-in-law)

Meadowside Laundry
Dysart Street O.S.ref. SJ909 881

This company was founded in 1902 as The Model Sanitary Laundry (Davenport) Ltd. but changed its name to The Model & Meadowside Laundries Ltd. some four years later, after taking over the Meadowside Laundry of Didsbury. The latter was situated alongside the River Mersey near the site presently occupied by the Waterside Hotel and Galleon Leisure Club. In 1910 Model & Meadowside took over The Ideal Laundry which was based at Mile End Lane.

During those early years domestic laundry work was collected by horse drawn van, but the effect of the First World War was to reduce the number of horses from 12 to 3 at Meadowside and by 1919 motor driven vans had been introduced. Some of these early motor vans were made up by placing bodies from old horse-drawn vans onto chassis from motor vehicle manufacturers such as Overland and Dodge.

For the next few years steady growth in the business took place, gaining the company a nationwide reputation for the quality of its work. It had now become one of the largest of its kind in the North West of England. The Second World War was to have another effect on the company in that work was allocated by a "Director of Laundry Services" appointed by the government. The Model & Meadowside Laundries allocation was to give a service mainly to the American Forces stationed at Poynton and take work from Western Command. Once again a war was responsible for depleting the firms transport, a large part of it being commandeered by the army. In order to build up the business after WW2 the laundry purchased several old Ford Vans from dealers and scrap yards and reconditioned them in their own garage. These vehicles became the company's main means of transport for the next 10 years.

Business expanded in the 1950's and 1960's. Laundering of stiff collars was a weekly occurrence, and linen and overall services to hotels and factories had been established. The fleet of vans operating over Greater Manchester and North Wales had risen to thirty. Also in the 1960's they further extended the business by opening six *Self Service* launderettes and dry cleaning shops.

In 1974 the company took over the Greenbank Laundry in Gatley. That same year an article appeared in the *Stockport Advertiser* of 4th July reporting that 'Smuts from the chimney on the Dysart Street plant was making life intolerable.' It is probable that the firm addressed this problem by changing to a gas fired boiler (which they were known to have had), the cone on the top of the chimney indicating that some form of modification had taken place.

By 1979 Meadowside Laundries Ltd., as it was now named, had a workforce of 152 people and was one of about 600 such companies left. Twenty years earlier there had been some 3000 or so companies but had been closed due to the use of man made fibres and the ever increasing use of domestic washing machines. Dry Cleaning eventually displaced laundering, and the need for some of the workshops and offices was no longer required. In 1995/6 most of the premises at Dysart Street, including the boiler house and chimney were demolished, leaving just a corner shop for dry cleaning and some commercial laundry services. The firm of Meadowside Laundries Ltd. ceased trading in September 1998, though a laundry business continued to operate there under the new ownership of Millbank Property Services who were based in Buxton. Meadowside had for a long time been associated with the Buxton firm. Dysart Street today provides housing in place of the demolished factory.

Information Source:-
Stockport Official Handbook for 1976

Factory with rail link south of Rose Hill

Park & Paterson Ltd.
Marple O.S.ref.SJ951 883

To a visitor, the last place one would expect to see a metal refining factory is in the centre of a respectable housing estate. But that is exactly where Messrs. Park & Paterson Ltd. find themselves. Not that they intruded, for this company were there long before the encroachment of houses. The company was founded in 1872 for the manufacturing and smelting of non-ferrous ingots. In 1901 they opened a new business in Salford, collecting, recovering and screening hundreds of tons of "skimmings" to cast into copper based ingots. In 1906 they expanded and moved to Miles Platting and in 1914 they moved to their present five-acre site in Marple where there had previously been a tallow factory, and before that the *Klondyke Brickworks*. This site not only possessed a furnace with chimney but also some artesian wells. With these facilities the company's progress was assured and it went from strength to strength to such an extent that in the 1950's business became so brisk that it was reported that 'ingots were being despatched still hot from the pour.' At that time rail transport was available, with Park & Paterson having their own branch line feeding north towards *Rose Hill Station*. This station is now a terminus and there is no longer a railway line south. Consequently the company utilises road transport for the movement of their goods. With the close proximity of the housing estate and Peacefield Primary School, Park & Paterson have been duty bound to respect the environment, and have invested thousands of pounds on modern furnace equipment and filtration systems. Melting is carried out in oil fired reverberatory and electric induction furnaces and all gaseous products are passed through bag filtration whereby metal oxides can be collected. Therefore there is minimum pollution escaping from the square sectioned brick chimney that stands about 80ft. tall and is heavily strapped over its entire height.

After 130 years since the company was founded, there are fourth generation members of the Paterson family on the Board of Directors.

One of Park & Paterson's customer's is the John Taylor bell foundry of Loughborough, the largest bell foundry in the world, and one of only two bell foundries still operating in Britain. Park & Paterson supply the Bronze alloy for casting into bells, some of which have been installed in town halls and cathedrals across the world.

Park and Paterson Ltd.
Park & Paterson Limited,
(ingot manufacturers since 1872).
Marple, Cheshire.
also at: Parkhead, Glasgow E.1.

The company letter head in 1976 when P & P Ltd. also had a branch at Glasgow

The latest company logo

NON-FERROUS INGOT MANUFACTURERS

The well strapped chimney, part shielded from view by conifers in a neighbouring garden

Information Sources:- *Stockport Official Handbook* for 1976
Kenneth Paterson

Pear New Mill

O.S.ref. SJ912 908

Constructed by Thomas Smethurst of Oldham, this was one of the last cotton spinning mills to be built during the final mill-building boom of the Edwardian era. The architects were A.H. Stott & Sons of Oldham, who had also designed the Stockport mills of *Broadstone* and *Houldsworth*. By 1908, when construction at Pear Mill started, mill design had benefited from over 100 years of development. (Arkwright's mill at Cromford was built in 1771). Consequently in Pear New Mill we witness a splendid building displaying both practical and ornamental features that have contributed to the mill being credited as a Grade II listed building. Originally planned as a double mill it would have been the largest ever, but the second half was never built. Work was initiated by the Pear Spinning Company, who ran into financial difficulties in 1912, and were wound up compulsorily, Mr. A.H. Stott being dismissed from the board on the grounds of extravagance. By this time only the shell of the building had been completed. A new company was formed with a different board of directors who appointed Philip S. Stott as a replacement for his brothers who were partners in A.H. Stott & Sons. The new company was called *Pear New Mill Ltd*. Even under new management the building costs still went over budget, but completion was finally achieved and production eventually commenced in July 1913.

Out of the seven storeys, the top five were for spinning with the lower two floors used for preparatory processes and storage. All the equipment installed in 1913 came from the famous firm of Platt Bros. of Oldham.

The floors were constructed from concrete, which was becoming available as an alternative to brick arches that hitherto had been the usual material of construction. The windows were large and numerous to allow maximum lighting and it was a feature to give the arches of the windows on the 7th floor a smaller radius than the arches above the windows of the floors below. The yellow brick band above the windows was a distinguishing mark of A.H. Stott mills of the period, but the styling tended towards the Baroque as opposed to the Italianate tradition of Stott's earlier mills like *Houldsworth*. The walls were in red Accrington Brick and there was much use of yellow brick and terra cotta decoration. Pear decoration was used throughout as a theme (the idea taken from the adjacent *Pear Tree Farm*) and can be seen on all corner turrets, the chimney plinth and the large pear capping the tower. The 195ft. tall chimney was circular in section, as chimneys tended to be in the early 20th century, and it incorporated all the features possible from plinth to crown. Although electricity from the public supply was available by 1912, Stott's favoured the classic steam engine for their power source, thus a huge engine with a design rating of 4500h.p. was installed by George Saxon Ltd. This was placed in an engine house which would have been centrally located had the second half of the mill been built. The engine was described as the *Manhattan Type* having two horizontal high pressure cylinders of 30 inches diameter and two vertical low pressure cylinders of 60 inches

"….much use of yellow brick and terra-cotta decoration"

diameter. The stroke was 4 feet 6 inches and the engine ran at 80r.p.m. but was only used to half of its capacity. It was used to drive a rope pulley of 22feet 6inches diameter with 76 grooves for 1¾ inch ropes. At 13 feet and 8 inches wide it was reckoned to be the widest rope pulley ever produced. The installation included four Lancashire boilers each 8½ feet diameter by 30 feet long and supplied by Tinker Shenton & Co.Ltd. of Hyde. Electrical power for lighting came from a Mather & Platt generator driven off the main engine. There was also a standby M & P generator driven by its own steam engine, which could supply electricity when the main engine was not running. Coal for the boilers was purchased locally from the Bredbury Colliery and water was taken from the adjacent River Goyt thereby eliminating the need for a lodge. However the mill had a reservoir on the tarred flat roof which was bordered by a 3ft parapet.

Output at Pear New Mill started with the spinning of Egyptian, American and Brazilian cotton, but ownership changed many times. It then moved into the spinning of fine cotton and was taken over by Combined Egyptian Mills Ltd. in 1929. In 1953 the company was re-named Combined English Mills (Spinners) Ltd. but 11 years later the mill was acquired by Viyella International. In the early 1950's some radical changes took place by replacing steam with electrical power. Also the 137,312 mule spindles were replaced by 33,636 ring spindles which required much less space occupying floors three and four only. Output level was maintained, but included the addition of cotton / rayon blends. Production ceased on 30th March 1978. The building has since been purchased and is let to various industrial units which include fabric pleating, bicycle manufacture, sportswear supply, ceramics and glassware. Pear New Mill now provides employment for approximately 120 people.

The plain east wall intended for abutment to the second half mill

Information Sources :-
Pear Mill, Stockport – An Edwardian Cotton Spinning Mill by R.N. Holden
(An article in *The Industrial Archaeological Review*, Vol.X, No2, Spring 1988)

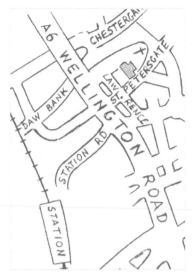

Petersgate Recreation Centre

O.S.ref. SJ894 902

Known originally as 'Public Baths and Wash-Houses,' the first building erected on this site, fronting Lawrence Street, was prompted by an interest in public hygiene following a cholera outbreak in Stockport in 1831. Apparently the opening of the baths on 8th August 1858 was a quiet affair, but the publicity must have been effective as 1,073 receipts were taken on the first day! Mostly it was mill workers who attended, to avail themselves of the facilities for which they had been pressing for some 20 years. The initial charge was 1d and for this some of the lads stayed all day. Later this was rectified and a time limit set. Popular as the baths were, it nevertheless became evident that the facilities were inadequate and some form of improvement was necessary. Swimming was not yet an option.

So after purchasing some land adjacent to the site, the council invited tenders to be submitted for an extension, offering a premium to whoever won the contract. In all 91 architects submitted plans including one from America. The winner was a Mr.Prestwich of Leigh, whose design, fronting St. Petersgate, was a three storey building in the Queen Anne Style.

Mr. Prestwich's design as illustrated in *The Stockport "Express" Record* of 1897

— · PUBLIC BATHS · —

DURING 1896, 67,000 persons used the Corporation Baths, St. Petersgate. The accommodation there is excellent, and the place is to be still further improved at a cost of about £3000. The fine Turkish bath is so popular that extension has been made necessary; whilst the sinking of a well at a cost of £2000, putting in a new boiler, &c., are in the improvement scheme.

The extension was opened ceremonially on 1st July 1886 by the mayor of that year, William Leigh, and all present were treated to Stockport's first swimming gala. In his opening speech the mayor mentioned that Daniel Adamson (famous for his part in the construction of the Manchester Ship Canal) had offered to supply the baths with "water from the blue Atlantic at one penny a ton". It is doubtful if that ever occurred or was even necessary as the site chosen for the baths was the source of one of the town's water supplies. Daniel Adamson was obviously a man not to miss an opportunity. The new baths included a gentleman's plunge bath, a ladies plunge bath (somewhat smaller) and a boys plunge bath. There were also 33 private baths and 3 Turkish Baths described as "luxurious with a handsome new smoke-room." The wash-house comprised 30 washing stalls, 4 hydro extractors, 24 irons, 30 drying horses and 3 mangles. One report stated that "indeed the City of Manchester has not such a smart set of baths". In 1928 a separate *Public Wash House* was opened in Bann Street allowing additional bathing facilities to be provided at the *Central Baths* in St. Petersgate. In 1933 the interior was entirely rebuilt, using the existing walls but with new steel roof trusses. The gentleman's plunge bath was reconstructed and that for the ladies followed soon after. Mixed bathing was still not permitted. Reconstruction of the small plunge pool followed much later in 1947 when the front elevation was radically changed from the earlier classic 3 storey building to a 2 storey flat roofed entrance with metal framed windows. At this time a new boiler by Cochran of Annan was installed and this was still in place at the time of closure some 46 years later. The boiler chimney was square in section and about 60ft. tall although a change in brick colour indicated that its height had probably been altered. Records state that the chimney had been repaired in 1970 and it was probably then that the pyramid shaped cowl was fitted. Later still the facilities were improved by the addition of a gymnasium, saunas and sunray treatment so that the building fully justified its new name of Petersgate Recreation Centre. Perhaps the most important community service provided by the centre was the facility given to school groups for training. Some 39 schools comprising 65,000 school children attended the baths each year. However popular the centre may have been it nevertheless possessed a Victorian interior and showed its age. Stockport required a state of the art facility to compete with other towns. Hence Grand Central Pools (comprising a 50 metre pool, seating for 500 spectators, and a health and fitness suite) was opened on 3rd April 1993 on Station Road to replace the Petersgate Recreation Centre after 135 years of service. The site was cleared in the Spring of 1996 and the area opened up for municipal gardens.

Victorian tiling on the upper parts of the internal walls

BATHS AND WASH-HOUSE

CENTRAL BATHS, ST. PETERSGATE : Comprising two large and one small swimming pool. Mixed bathing daily, 8d. and 10d. Recently constructed private hot bath suite for ladies and gentlemen—charge 8d. Comfortable Turkish Baths, Gents : Mon., Wed., Fri., and Sat. Ladies : Tues., and Thurs. 4/-. Up-to-date Sun-Ray Tonic Baths, separate sections for ladies and gentlemen, in charge of experienced operators. Open daily, charge 1/6d., book of 7 tickets, 10/-.

BRANCH BATH, GORTON ROAD, REDDISH : One large pool and private hot bath facilities for both sexes.

PUBLIC WASH-HOUSE, BANN STREET, STOCKPORT : Modern electric washing machines, with hydro-extractors and drying horses.

An extract from the *Stockport Official Handbook* for 1953

A view of the large pool taken in the last week of its use; March 1993

Information Source:- Stockport Local Heritage Library ref.S/R82

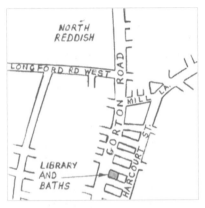

Reddish Baths
O.S.ref. SJ896 939

For the residents of Reddish the opening of the Public Baths on Gorton Road on 27th May 1908 was a major triumph, as they had been campaigning for a long time for a local facility instead of having to travel into Stockport. They were rewarded with a fine Edwardian building designed by architects Dixon and Potter that included a Fire Station and Free Public Library as well as the baths. The land for the site had been donated by the owners of Greg's Mill and the opening ceremony was performed by Henry Bell, the Mayor of Stockport. Unfortunately this triumphal opening did not herald a trouble-free future for the baths; the expected attendance never materialised. In 1950 the Mayor (Alderman G.W. Piper) stated that "something needed to be done to encourage people to use the baths to relieve the overcrowding at St. Petersgate." Later that year a number of extensions were constructed to provide "more space, more modern showers including the latest type of foot shower, and lavatory accommodation." These still failed to attract the desired number of users and criticism was voiced in 1969 that "there is a lack of dressing room facilities, particularly in the upper gallery where women have to change with very little privacy." Thereafter the baths were regularly being reviewed by the council who threatened to close them, as they were uneconomical and out of date. In 1996 Stockport Council were reported to be considering a bid to build new swimming baths in the Reddish area with assistance from the National Lottery. At one stage there was a proposal to re-site the baths in Houldsworth Mill as part of the redevelopment plans there, but this never came to reality. Then in 1999 the future of the baths again became uncertain, as they had to close due to boiler failure. Once again a reprieve was secured and a new boiler commissioned, but this time a new concept in boiler design was installed i.e. a mobile boiler. This took the form of a container (as one sees transported on lorries) and was installed outside in a compound where it was self contained complete with oil fuel tank and flue gas funnel. Consequently the square section brick chimney that exhausted the fumes from the previous boilers became redundant.

The original boiler for the heating of the baths was fuelled by coke, but there had been a switch to oil by the time the last internal installation failed in 1999. The library and fire station had their own heating arrangements.

The fire station was located in the centre of the complex and was constructed with a hayloft and stalls for three horses. Quarters for the firemen were provided on the first and second floors. It was not until June 1928 that Reddish Fire Station received its first motor driven fire engine and it was another three years after that before all the horses had been retired. This fire station was a sub branch to the headquarters in Mersey Square and served the community well for more than 50 years. Following the opening of a new fire service headquarters at Whitehill and a new sub-station at King Street, both the Reddish Branch and the Mersey Square station were closed after 14th April 1967 when the new ones were opened. The fire station on Gorton Road then became the Community Centre for Reddish.

The library continues to give service from its position at the north end of the complex where it was originally planned.

Information Sources:- *A History of Stockport Fire Brigade* by Arthur Smith
Newspaper cuttings at Stockport Local History Library

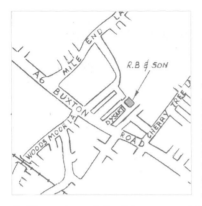

Robert Bailey & Son
O.S.ref. SJ909 881

This site was originally occupied from about 1910 by a towelling manufacturer called The David Dickie Towel Co.Ltd. The company was in business for about 23 years at Dysart Street before moving out to Australia, allegedly taking with it some of the staff of *Moorites* (as people from Great Moor were known locally). The vacancy was taken up by the firm of Robert Bailey & Son who wished to expand its already established business of manufacturing surgical dressings. Originally from Lancashire, Robert Bailey set up his works at Marriott Street, Stockport about 1912 and he set up an office in Southampton Row, London. This was suitably in time to gear up to supply the enormous demand for surgical dressings required during the Great War. In addition to manufacturing bandages, cotton wool, gauzes and lint, the company also produced First Aid Cabinets that they marketed with the trade name "Zorbo". By chance they acquired the Dysart Street Works in time to meet the demands of the Second World War and from then on they ran the two centres in Stockport up until 1998 when the Marriott Street Works was closed. At Dysart Street the chimney was once about 140ft. tall but when the photograph was taken it had been reduced to about 25 ft. tall. This occurred some time after 1956 following a change over from coal burning to oil when different boilers were introduced. It was round in section and originally served a Lancashire boiler which was used mainly for space heating, but was also used in the processing of material in a department of the factory called the Boric Room. It was there for example where lint would be transformed from the bleached white colour to the familiar pink product.

In the 1980's the workforce was about 150 strong and about 30% of the products went for export to all parts of the world. The trade name for their products was *Steraid*. In the early part of the year 2000 they were subject to a takeover by a company called Millpledge Healthcare and from that time on the factory in Dysart Street was re-named as Robert Bailey (UK) Ltd. and employed only 49 people. Two years later this company went into receivership and closed down on 27th September 2002. Within a short space of time the premises were demolished and the building of a housing estate, comprising 24 three-bedroom properties, was commenced in January 2003.

A company advert from the 1920's

Information Sources:- Stockport Local History Library
Geoff. Hulme – ex employee Robert Bailey & Son

Royal Oak Brewery
O.S.ref. SJ898 895

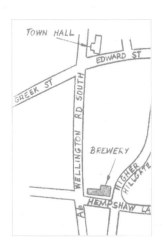

Brewing of ale developed from the Royal Oak Inn on Higher Hillgate in the 1840's. In 1875 after a fire, new premises were sought and the building we know today was found – a former cotton mill. One of the early brewers was Daniel Clifton who traded as *Daniel Clifton & Co. Ales*. In 1885 he set up his *Mineral Water Manufactory* on the adjacent site, the words describing this being visible in the brickwork above the windows of the top floor. (See photograph below). Artesian wells were sunk purely for the production of the mineral waters. The Manchester Brewery took over the business in the 1920's, followed by Whitbreads in 1943, but brewing ceased at the Royal Oak in 1957. The premises at one time housed a steam engine called Clara. The chimney for the boiler room was round in section and about 60 to 70ft. high. Today the premises are owned by a property company who let sections out to a variety of industrial users.

Information Sources:-
A History of Stockport Breweries by Mike Ogden
Portrait of Stockport by John Creighton

Advert from the Stockport Directory of 1907

School Street

Hazel Grove, O.S.ref. SJ922 866

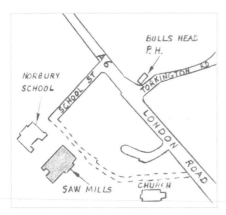

The first ordnance survey map to show any building on this site was for 1934 when saw mills were indicated. George Fryer Ltd. were the first known occupiers, listed as joinery manufacturers, and they were there from about 1924 until 1939 making furniture at their mill known as Norbury Works. In 1940 the name changed to S & F Fryer Ltd. and with the occurrence of the Second World War a change of output was forced on them by the government. The company's expertise was utilised for making aircraft frames, particularly for the RAF *Mosquito* Bomber which had been designed to have a wooden frame, thereby avoiding the use of metals, which were scarce in wartime. S & F Fryer Ltd. carried on at School Street as *Aeronautical Woodworkers* until 1955.

In 1956 the premises were taken over by S.E.I. (Salford Electrical Instruments) Ltd., a subsidiary of the giant General Electric Company. S.E.I. who were based in Silk Street, Salford were a well established company with branches already in Heywood, Middleton, and Stockport (Kingston Mill). The acquisition of the School Street premises became the Hazel Grove Branch for S.E.I. where they manufactured new electronic devices called *semiconductors*. Thus began the story of a firm that seemed to be forever changing its name. In 1958 the name S.E.I., at Hazel Grove, was changed to G.E.C. Semiconductors. The initial development of semiconductors within G.E.C. had taken place at their research laboratories in Wembley, Middlesex and they retained those laboratories for some time, but concentrated production at the School Street factory. Not content with School Street for the long term, G.E.C. also purchased Broadstone Mills in Reddish, predicting (erroneously) an even greater expansion of production in the near future. Nevertheless production did run at a high level and some 1400 people were employed by G.E.C. Semiconductors at Hazel Grove during the early 1960's.

Most of the production operatives for that type of work were female as the main attribute for delicate electronic assembly was dexterity. By 1962 G.E.C. Semicoductors had combined with the semiconductor division of Mullard and so a new company was formed called Associated Semiconductor Manufacturers, or A.S.M. as the local people described the firm. When the G.E.C. interest diminished and the parent company of Mullard (Philips Electronics) assumed overall control, the name A.S.M. gave way to *Mullard Hazel Grove*. The new management looked upon Broadstone Mill in a different light from G.E.C. and soon sold it off - semiconductors were never produced there. Philips realised the premises at School Street did not offer the right environment for the future production of semicoductors and looked for a new site. Subsequently the firm moved into a new purpose built factory on Pepper Road, off Bramhall Moor Lane in 1970. The company was still known as Mullard Hazel Grove when it vacated School Street, but has since been called Philips Components and then later called Philips Semiconductors and has become one of Stockport's major employers.

Since 1970 the premises at School Street have been let out for various purposes from a roller skating rink to housing a double glazing manufacturer. The chimney at School Street was never very prominent but survived the occupancy of all the owners. It was square in section and about 50ft. tall and served the boilers for space heating.

Information Source :- The author and Tony Cummings (ex work colleague)

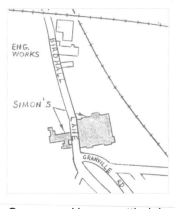

Simon Engineering Group
O.S.ref. SJ878 883

For nearly three quarters of a century there would have been few local people that were not aware of the firm of *Simon* on Bird Hall Lane, Cheadle Heath. To most people it was the name *Simon-Carves* that first came to mind but there were in fact nine businesses that formed the Simon Group. It all started in 1860 when 24 year old Henry Simon arrived in Manchester following his education at a Swiss Polytechnic. Originally from Germany, Henry settled in Manchester as a consulting engineer, a practice that involved extensive travel and providing Henry with an insight into many industrial processes. He saw the opportunity to improve on two processes in particular, and as a result he established two firms. The first was Henry Simon Ltd. founded in 1878 for the design and installation of roller flour-milling equipment. This virtually revolutionised the industry of flour milling, which hitherto in England was based on the age-old system of using millstones. Then in 1880, in partnership with Francois Carves, a distinguished French coke-oven engineer, the firm of Simon-Carves was established to develop the manufacture of by-product coke ovens. Between them they saw the opportunity of manufacturing coke with much improved efficiency and utilising the by-products with far less pollution of the environment. Both businesses were formed into limited companies around 1896/7.

Henry Simon was a good citizen of Manchester. He supported the Hallé Society and Orchestra in their time of need, took the lead in establishing the Manchester Crematorium (only the second in the country), and gave substantial financial support for the building of a new physics laboratory at Owens College where he was invited to lay the foundation stone. He lived in Didsbury near the banks of the River Mersey in a house called *Lawnhurst* and died in1899 age 64, having brought up eight children. The second eldest of these children (Ernest) chaired the company from 1910, leading the firm into International recognition.

The Cheadle Heath works were opened in 1926 and by 1930 all the office staff from Mount Street in Manchester had been transferred too. By this time the company had expanded into four new areas; coal washing, conveying department for grain handling, chemical plant for sulphuric acid manufacture, and a boiler department. By 1934 all nine businesses were in operation. These included the engineering works (where nearly all the flour milling machinery was built), a soap machinery department, and Turbine Gears Ltd. (a company acquired with the object of filling the works in times of depression). They also owned Tyresoles Ltd. (a company involved in the re-treading of rubber tyres). The latter firm was however situated in Wembley, Middlesex. During WW2 90% of the Cheadle Heath output was allocated to armaments and industrial production for war factories. After the war the order books soon became full again and by 1946 there were 3972 employees. By 1953 Simon-Carves employed 4555 people and Henry Simon more than 3000. Training at Simon's was second to none, and apprenticeships gained there were highly valued.

Looking west from Granville Road

Ernest Simon also led an active public life and he became Lord Mayor of Manchester when he was only age 42. He was a Liberal M.P. on two occasions but transferred to the Labour movement in 1947. In the mid 1920's he presented the City of Manchester with the gift of 250 acres of land and a manor house at Wythenshawe. Manchester responded by granting Ernest the Freedom of the City and Westminster recommended him for a peerage, which he duly accepted as Lord Simon of Wythenshawe. Ernest died in 1972 age 93. By then the company based at Cheadle Heath was known as The Simon Engineering Group. In 1997 The Simon Engineering Group celebrated its centenary but soon afterwards underwent major restructuring resulting in its complete withdrawal from Cheadle Heath. Today, locally we are left only with Simon Carves Ltd. in new offices in Cheadle Hulme where they are engaged in Chemical plant design and process plant which could range from food processing to nuclear decontamination. Flour-milling engineering was taken on by the firm of Satake UK Ltd. who, for a brief period, occupied the offices vacated by Henry Simon Ltd. on Birdhall Lane. Satake UK Ltd. later relocated to Bredbury.

In the 1990's there were three chimneys to be seen within the various Simon premises. One served the office block where research and development took place. Here too was the tower (currently under threat of demolition) where flour-milling trials were carried out. The second chimney served a glass-fronted boiler room situated on the corner of Granville Road and Birdhall Lane; all since gone. The third chimney and the only one to survive into the 21st century belonged to Simon Carves Ltd. who were situated on the west side of Birdhall Lane. These premises are now part occupied by Stockport Direct Services, contractor to Stockport M.B.C. The front of this building includes a stone mounted above a lintel with the initials **SC** moulded into it; probably the only tangible evidence that Simon Carves once existed here. The remaining *Lawnhurst* Industrial Estate is a reminder of Henry Simon.

Information Sources:- *In search of a Grandfather* by Brian Simon
The Simon Engineering Group – Northern Publishing Co.Ltd.

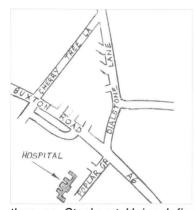

Stepping Hill Hospital
O.S.ref. SJ912 876

The first buildings on this site were built as accommodation wards by *The Stockport Union* to ease the congestion that existed at the Union Workhouse on Shaw Heath. George Neil Andrew, Chairman of the Board of Guardians, laid the foundation stone on 5th October 1903. Some two years later (7th December 1905) the chairman also officially opened the hospital, which was known then as *Stockport Union Infirmary*. Separate plaques commemorating these two events can be seen in the entrance hall to the hospital. At the opening ceremony it was stated that Shaw Heath had accommodation for 850 people, but on the Sunday before the opening of the new hospital there were 1050 inmates of whom 60 were tramps. So it was with some relief and justifiable pride that the Board of Guardians was able to declare its new hospital open. It comprised four pavilions, maternity wards, an administration block, a nurses' home, and a laundry, and was built in such a way that extensions could easily be carried out. The entrance to the hospital was off Poplar Grove (as it still is) and that is how the premises were referred to. For example if someone died at the hospital the death would be registered as having occurred at No.26 Poplar Grove and no reference to the hospital made whatsoever. Another sign of the times was the tradition carried out by the male officers of the institution in holding an Annual Smoking Concert when a pianist, singers and a humorist would provide entertainment. In 1914 it was recorded that the Steward on that occasion was presented with 'a solid oak smoking cabinet well stocked with all the good things desired by a smoker;' a far cry from today's expectations and guidelines associated with an institution promoting health.

The year 1914 saw an extension to the nurses' home but more importantly it was the year when the Great War commenced. This significantly affected Stepping Hill, for, as with many hospitals during the war, it came under military rule. Arrangements were made to transfer patients from Stepping Hill back to the Workhouse on Shaw Heath so that wounded soldiers could be accommodated at the former.

The number of patients at Stepping Hill increased from 336 in January 1915 to 439 by August 1916 of which 250 were wounded or gassed soldiers and sailors. By November 1916 three-thousand patients had been admitted since the commencement of the war. Until 1918 the hospital ambulances were horse drawn, but during that year the first suggestion was voiced for a motor driven ambulance to be considered as a replacement for "a tired old horse". When World War II started the hospital was once again requested to make preparations – this time to be ready for emergencies at a few minutes notice. Although patient numbers had increased considerably from 1,900 in 1930 to 6,000 in 1940, there were in fact many empty beds at Stepping Hill during WW II. As in the Great War many patients had been transferred to Shaw Heath and there was also a shortage of nurses. However the latter situation was alleviated partially by the offer of both doctors and nurses from the medical corps of the American Army. In March 1944 it was reported that over the previous twelve months more patients had been treated and more operations performed than ever before in the history of the hospital.

The year 1948 saw the beginning of the National Health Service and Stepping Hill became part of that, finally throwing aside the stigma of being a *Poor Law Hospital*, by which it was labelled, even though the Board of Guardians had transferred their responsibilities to the Public Assistance Committee of the Corporation back in 1930. As an increased level of service from the N.H.S. became necessary, so the need arose for expansion at the hospital. Around 1966 the building of a new Maternity and Midwifery Block was begun. This was at that time quite separate from the existing buildings and was the first major (120 beds) hospital construction planned since 1910. Since then so many additions have taken place that volunteer guides have been recruited to escort people around this vast complex. One of the more notable additions was a new hospital laundry opened in October 1976 capable of dealing with 150,000 articles per week. This was the most modern hospital laundry to be found in the North West at that time.

Another major addition was a new Accident and Emergency Unit that was opened in October 1996 replacing the department previously located at Stockport Infirmary which closed that year. Then in 1999 The Tree House Hospital was opened, specifically to cater for children. In 1998 there were in excess of 3000 employees working at the hospital which by then had been given the title of *Stockport Acute Services NHS Trust*. Some 5600 cars are reckoned to travel to and from the site each day, a situation that presents the hospital with an on-going parking problem. This vast hospital complex has come a long way from its beginnings as No.26 Poplar Grove, when the boiler house and chimney were situated centrally between the four pavilions. The modern boiler house is located on the south west edge of the site and is just one part of an energy efficient power plant, providing essential services for space heating, the kitchens, the laundry, and sterilisation. Its importance is paramount, and in order to cope with all foreseeable circumstances the boilers are able to operate using either gas or oil. The present chimney at Stepping Hill was built in the 1960's and is one of the more modern to be seen in Stockport, being parallel sided and built from concrete.

Information Source :- *Stockport Advertiser* reports 1905 to 1999

Stockport Infirmary

O.S.ref. SJ895 899

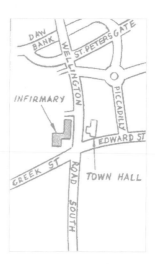

The Memorial Extension with old and new chimneys
seen from Edgeley Station Car Park

The building on Wellington Road South was first opened in 1834, but the origins of an Infirmary in Stockport start around 1774 when a surgeon, James Briscall, at his own expense, established a medical practice on the site of The Thatched House Tavern on Churchgate, that provided a free dispensary. But as the town's industry switched from silk to cotton spinning the need for a purpose built public dispensary became increasingly apparent, and so the *Daw Bank Dispensary and House of Recovery* came into being – opened in 1792. Extra wards (paid for by Peter Marsland the owner of Park Mills) were added in 1799 for fever patients, but it was soon recognised that even larger premises were needed to fulfil the town's requirements. Indeed Daw Bank contained no surgical beds.

Hence Stockport Infirmary was opened on the 24th July 1833 on land donated by Lady Vernon. The building was designed by Richard Lane in classical Greek Style and stood little wider than the four columns that support the central portico that we see today in the centre of the building.

THE INFIRMARY, STOCKPORT.

A postcard sent
in 1912

In order to cope with increasing outbreaks of infectious diseases such as cholera, the South Wing was added in 1870, the foundation stone being laid by Richard Sykes, industrial bleacher and a previous Mayor of Stockport. However by 1882 cases of smallpox and cholera were no longer accepted at the infirmary and went to the isolation hospital situated on Dialstone Lane. Several building phases followed: Reconstruction of the wards in 1885 as separate pavilions, and opening of the North Wing in 1900. Then in 1918 the King Edward VII Memorial Extension was added which included a new outpatient department and accident ward. It was about this time that new central heating and hot water plant was installed and this probably dates the octagonal section chimney. The foundation stone for the Memorial Extension was laid by Lt.Col.Alan Sykes (grandson of Richard) and later in 1938, when he was Sir Alan Sykes, he opened the Centenary Extension on the north side of the hospital. Sir Alan gave 50 years service to the infirmary and became Chairman of the Board of Governors. Other members of the Sykes family also served the infirmary well. Sir Alan's father, Captain Thomas Hardcastle Sykes was a committee member from 1864 and later was Hon. Treasurer until his death in April 1901. The founder of the Sykes family business, William, was Vice President of the early dispensary in 1819.

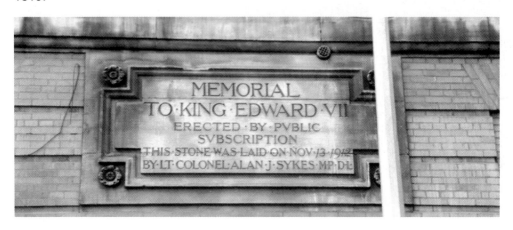

In addition to treating patients in two world wars the hospital came to prominence on 4th June 1967 when survivors were rushed in after a British Midland holiday plane crashed in the town. This disaster resulted in 72 people losing their lives, all of whom were either passengers or crew on the plane that was returning from Palma, Majorca with 84 people on board. The infirmary was only a few hundred yards from the crash point and in direct line of the flight path. It was fortunate to be able to receive the injured and not be part of an even bigger disaster. Some time later a vain attempt was made to have the title *Royal* bestowed upon the infirmary in recognition of both the service given at the time and the bravery of the pilot who survived. Stockport Infirmary closed in April 1996 having served as a hospital for 162 years. From that date all the hospital services for the area were provided at Stepping Hill. The infirmary buildings were put up for sale, advertising the fact that they were Grade II listed, but developers seemed reluctant to act and the premises were untouched for over two years. When development did take place, the front elevation was preserved and the opportunity was taken to demolish several incongruous extensions. As completion extended into the 21st century the building was renamed as *Millennium House*, and speculators expected a hotel and conference centre. Instead Millennium House, as from September 2002, became *The Pensions Service*, a government controlled service that potentially could employ 500 people serving a large part of the North West.

The two chimneys seen in the photograph of the Memorial Extension were demolished during the development phase and the building itself was detached from the main structure that fronted Wellington Road South by removing link corridors. The Memorial Extension was renamed *Arden Buildings* and converted into apartments.

Stockport Infirmary shortly before closure

Information Source:- *Stockport Infirmary, A Short History* by Charles Smith

The Chocolate Factory

O.S.ref. SJ881 903

There has never been one lasting title for the premises on Brighton Road, but as most of its life has been associated with confectionery, I am referring to it as *The Chocolate Factory*. It was built (probably in the 1880's) for Henry Faulder, a grocer, registered in Bridge Street as a dealer in tea, preserves, marmalade and confectionery. In 1893 Henry Faulder & Co.Ltd. were listed as *Wholesale Grocers, Confectioners and Fruit Preservers* having premises at Bridge Street, Heaton Norris and premises called *The Model Fruit Preserving Works* at Norris Bank. This latter description is the first positive reference to be found in the trade directories to the premises on Brighton Road. By 1895 the factory was known as *The Silverpan Fruit Preserving Works* and it was intermittently called this until 1938. Because of Henry Faulder's other enterprises, both titles and addresses would change from time to time. By 1905 Faulder had charge of a Cocoa Works in Warren Street, Portwood; the Preserve Works in Norris Bank; and Squirrel Confectionery at Hallam Mill in Heaviley. In addition to that he set up general offices on St. Petersgate and probably had other offices in part of Wellington Mill, since Silverpan was registered there in 1924/5. In 1917, as illustrated on a letterhead, The Chocolate Factory was known as Henry Faulder & Co.Ltd. though Henry Faulder himself had died 10 years before. Another change came in the 1930's when the factory was called The Squirrel Chocolate Works.

At the end of 1936 Cadbury acquired The Chocolate Factory for use as a distribution depot for the joint products of Cadbury and Fry, with whom they had merged back in 1919. Cadbury viewed this acquisition as a real coup as it was one of the largest and most important developments in depot distribution and according to their publication, *The Bournville Works Magazine,* would "lead to considerable economies in operation, and to a greatly increased efficiency". Hitherto both Cadbury and Fry ran separate delivery services from centres in Manchester and Liverpool, and so the new depot in Stockport that opened on 20th September 1937 was described as performing a 'four-in-one-role.'

The *Bournville Works Magazine* also described the building it had purchased in Stockport and mentioned the railway siding that adjoined the line on the Cheshire Lines Railway: "the building is eminently suitable for depot work and has a total floor area of 80,000 square feet, consisting of stock room, offices, canteen, and outbuildings. The rail deck is totally enclosed and is inside the building; the road deck can deal with twelve vans simultaneously". The remainder of the article gave a glowing account of Stockport and its environs. Messrs. Cadbury carried out their distribution activities from Stockport for nearly 50 years, selling the site in 1986. Since then the premises, known as Brighton Road Industrial Estate, have been managed by various property dealing companies, letting out units for warehouse purposes or manufacturing. When first built, the chimney was about 150ft. high and had one of the most ornate crowns to be seen, made up of two oversailers occupying the top 10 to 15ft. The lower of the two oversailers projected out the most on four fluted corbels to each side of the octagon, providing a large collar supporting another 6 to 7ft. of chimney topped with a smaller oversailer of a similar design. Of all the chimneys remaining in Stockport the one at The Chocolate Factory was one of the finest until the year 2001 when the top crown was removed, leaving a plain looking chimney of octagonal cross section that was typical for the 1880's when it was constructed.

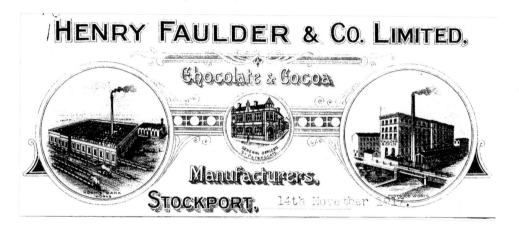

From a letterhead dated 14th November 1917, showing the Brighton Road premises at Norris Bank on the left, the Cocoa Works at Portwood on the right, and Faulder's offices on St. Petersgate in the centre.

Information Sources:-
    Stockport Local History Library – file on Henry Faulder
    Cadbury Information and Library Service

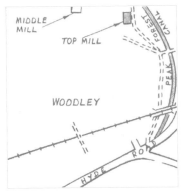

Top Mill
Woodley – O.S.ref. SJ935 925

In the early to middle 19th century an interesting clutch of mills in Woodley were built for a variety of purposes including corn grinding to cotton weaving. Three of these mills stretched in a line between the Peak Forest Canal and the River Tame and were respectively called Top, Middle, and Bottom Mill, the latter subsequently called Botany Mill. Where these three mills appear on maps they are described as woollen mills, but mostly they commenced their working lives as bone mills for fertilizer production. In 1850 Top Mill was owned by John Leigh. Some time later John Lees Buckley became the owner, not only of Top Mill, but also of Middle Mill, Bottom Mill and Wood Mill which lay further down the valley. Once established John Lees Buckley became successful and was described in the Stockport Trade Directory for 1872 as *Woolcarder and Hatter*. He re-built several of his mills, including Top Mill in 1872, extending it five years later. In the second half of the 19th century the Buckley family became the major employer in Woodley, and were known locally for their participation in public services. For several years John Lees was Chairman of the Bredbury Local Board, and one of his sons, Thomas, was four times Chairman of Bredbury and Romiley Urban District Council. All of the Buckley family were members of the Methodist Church, John Lees being a preacher, and his son, Samuel, organist.

In 1909 Buckley's sold Top Mill to Messrs. Goodman & Wagstaffe who used the mill for the manufacture of leather gloves. Then in 1934 Messrs. Macphail & Kay took over the premises, also for the manufacture of leather gloves. Macphail & Kay were described in the Stockport Trade Directory for 1954 as *Chamois Leather Manufacturers and Dressers*. They remained at Top Mill until closure in 1990. Sadly a year later, before John Macphail could manage to sell the mill, thieves stole every roof slate and removed the copper pipe and brass fittings. At the time (June 1991) an estimate of £12,000 was quoted to furnish the mill with a new roof without which it was unsaleable. So it was never repaired and consequently all that remains of Top Mill is a square section chimney standing about 60 to 70ft. high amongst the ruins.

ELECTRICAL ENGINEERS AND CONTRACTORS
Godson's (Romiley) Ltd., 22 Compstall Road, Romiley. Tel. WOO 2027.

ENGINEERS (LOCOMOTIVE)
Davies & Metcalfe Ltd., Injector Works, Romiley.

ESTATE AGENTS
Roberts & Roberts (G. C. Roberts, F.I.A.S. (Consultant), C. D. G. Roberts, F.R.I.C.S., F.A.I., R. P. le Poidevin, A.R.I.C.S., A.A.I.), 4 Compstall Road, Romiley. Tel. WOO 4037.

FISH, GAME & POULTRY
Mellor, G., 58 Compstall Rd., Romiley. Tel. WOO 2385.

FISH FRYERS
Fowden, 16 Hyde Road, Woodley.
Wilson, F., 5 Compstall Rd., Romiley.

FRUITERERS, FLORISTS AND GREENGROCERS
Dace, Mrs. E. M., 41 Compstall Rd., Romiley.
Fieldings, 6 Hyde Road, Woodley.
Jamieson, W., 8 Cherry Tree Lane, Romiley.
Mellor, G., 58 Compstall Road,

Romiley. Tel. WOO 2385.
Romiley Fruit Stores (The), 24 Stockport Road, Romiley.
Woods (Florists) Ltd., 16 Compstall Road, Romiley.

FUNERAL FURNISHERS
Jordan, E. (Limousines for Weddings), 2 Stockport Rd., Bredbury. Tel. WOO 2514.

GARAGES
Bridgeside Garage Ltd., Stockport Road, Romiley. Tel. WOO 2802.

GLOVE MANUFACTURERS
Goodman & Gooder (Romiley) Ltd., Bridge Works, Romiley. Tel. WOO 2071.
MacPhail & Kay Ltd., Top Mill, Woodley. Tel. 2021.

GROCERS AND PROVISION MERCHANTS
Aspinall, A. & T. (Bakers and Confectioners), 6 Cherry Tree Lane, Romiley.
Brown, J. H., 144 Stockport Road, Romiley.
Caw, P. L., 50 Hyde Road, Woodley.

Advert from The Hyde & District Directory for 1964/5

171

Information Sources:- *Woodley and Greave* by Roy Frost and Ian Simpson
Stockport Local Heritage Library ref.S/J46

Unity Mill
Woodley – O.S.ref. SJ939 930

This four storey mill, situated on the south east bank of the Peak Forest Canal, was known originally as Trianon Mill. It was built for cotton spinning, but by 1893 it was being used as a rubber works for The Hyde Imperial Rubber Co. However in the early 1900's the mill reverted back to cotton spinning under the new owners of Mayall & Massey who were listed in the trade directories as Cotton Doublers. Messrs. Mayall & Massey continued in business at Unity Mill until 1952. In 1953 the chemical firm of Norman Evans & Rais Ltd. moved from Cheadle into Unity Mill, in order to expand its manufacture of industrial enzymes, used in the baking and brewing industries. This was taken over by Associated British Maltsters in 1964 who in turn were bought by RTZ Chemicals in 1986. Three years later this became part of Rhone-Poulenc and it remains as such, though Rhone-Poulenc reorganised its chemicals, fibres and polymers business to form a new speciality chemicals company called *Rhodia* of which the site at Woodley is a part. On this 16 acre site there are 140 people employed in the manufacture of microbiological enzymes for food and industrial applications. As well as housing the enzymes production plant, Unity Mill contains the laboratories and the *Northern Administration Centre* for Rhodia. Steam is an essential part of the process and is also used for sterilising and space heating. It is generated by two oil-fired boilers supplied by Joseph Adamson of Hyde. The chimney serving these boilers is octagonal in cross section and probably dates back to the 19th century. It currently stands about 100 ft. high but is believed to have been shortened when it was lined and fitted with a cowl. It has been girded with iron straps at approximately 6ft. intervals and has been well treated with linseed oil to prevent ingress of water. These factors probably contributed to its survival. The factory is still surrounded by open countryside and enjoys its own bowling green. The company, appreciative of its situation, exercises great consideration for the environment and takes many precautions to keep its waste and emissions to a minimum.

Information Sources:- *Woodley and Greave* by Roy Frost and Ian Simpson
Pat Hill and Tom Delaney – Rhodia Ltd.

Victoria Dyeworks

O.S.ref. SJ900 894

Map from around 1959
showing the factory with three
worker's cottages that were
later demolished

A relatively small business, Victoria Dyeworks was established in the mid 19th century by John Hazeldine, a resident of Heaviley, for the manufacturing of yarns. By 1891 Oswald Hazeldine had taken over, and the title remained under his name until the 1970's. The premises were then purchased by Malbern Properties, who let the buildings out, dividing them initially into nine units. A variety of businesses occupied these units at different stages, amongst them were Betta Bedrooms and J.D. Mellor & Sons, the latter being engineers to the boiler trade. More recently several firms have taken up part ownership, providing an interesting cross section of occupations. The Hempshaw Motor Co. established itself there in 1976, occupying the unit that was once used as the machine shop for the dye works. To make way for the motor company's yard three cottages, which had originally been built for rental by the dye workers, were demolished. Another company that was there for many years was Newcol Ltd., pigment manufacturers to the rubber industry. The square sectioned chimney belongs to that part of the premises owned by Neil Slinger, upholsterers, who went there in 1991. The chimney standing about 45/50ft. high, was thought to have served a boiler in the original dye works, was slightly reduced in height in the latter half of 2002.

Even this small chimney was
endowed with features

An advert from the *Stockport Directory* of 1887

Information Source:-   Neil Slinger
Hempshaw Motors

Wear Mill

O.S.ref. SJ890 902

Built in 1790 by John Collier, a cotton manufacturer, the mill was progressively extended such that today it has the widest range of period structures of any mill site remaining in Greater Manchester, and now has Grade II listed building status. It was situated beside the River Mersey in order to take advantage of the water-power. Part of the original 1790 wheelhouse still exists at the western end of the complex, and the second oldest structure, built in 1831, stands at the eastern end partly bridged by one of the arches of Stockport Railway Viaduct. The extension to this latter structure features a type of cast iron floor beam called the Hodgkinson Beam. Introduced in 1831 as a stronger but lighter beam than those previously used in so called fireproof mills where there had been a series of collapses of cast iron beams and columns in the early part of the 19th century. The weaving shed, built in the mid 19th century and situated partly beneath the arches of the viaduct, features the saw tooth or *north light* roof where glazing was only used in the steeper north facing side of the ridge. This type of construction later became very common. Another building, re-built in 1884, features unusually narrow longitudinal vaults mounted on heavy transverse cast iron beams designed to minimise any thrust from the arches being transmitted to the walls.

After John Collier's ownership the mill was taken over in 1824 by Thomas Fernley and remained ostensibly in the hands of the Fernley family throughout the 19th century. Thomas Fernley & Sons were involved in both spinning and weaving, and suffered more than one fire; one on May Day 1843 claiming three lives. It is significant to note that the fire brigade at that time was led not by a chief fire officer but by the Comptroller of Police. By the end of the 19th century the mill belonged to The Fine Spinners and Doublers Association and it was running 60,000 spindles by 1892. *Wear Mill* is frequently referred to as *Weir Mill* and it is not known which is correct. However from the knowledge that John Collier possessed two mills, facing each other across the Mersey with a weir strung between them, the latter of the two names would seem to be the more apt. In more recent times the mill has been occupied by a range of small businesses, a familiar name amongst them being Slimtru (Clothing Manufacturers). The chimney (about 120ft. tall and octagonal) was demolished in the autumn of 1995.

Views showing the 1831 building partly beneath the railway viaduct

Information Sources:-
Cotton Mills in Greater Manchester by M.Williams & D.A.Farnie
A History of Stockport Fire Brigade by Arthur Smith

Welkin Mill
O.S.ref. SJ912 914

A map from the 1960's period showing the original loop in the River Goyt before it was diverted to make way for the motorway that replaced the Tiviot Dale to Bredbury railway line

The site on which Welkin Mill was built, was originally part of Elm Tree Farm, Bredbury. In 1907 the Ark Ring Spinning Co. Ltd. was formed with Mr. Joseph Linney, the owner of Elm Tree Farm, as one of its directors. The company called the building Ark Mill and in order to advertise its presence had the word **Ark** imprinted on two sides of the chimney. The word is still visible. Designed by J.A. Ashton of Altrincham, Ark Mill was amongst the first to use electricity to drive its machinery by generating its own power. The generators were driven by steam turbines, the boiler house being similar to that of a conventional steam powered mill. The fine round section chimney is typical of the early 20th century chimneys and today is one of the most visible in the Stockport area, being just a few metres away from the M6 motorway. However, before the photographs were taken the chimney was about 20ft. taller.

Unfortunately for Joseph Linney, Ark Mill was a personal financial disaster and he was obliged to sell Elm Tree Farm in 1909. The mill later came into the ownership of the Lancashire Cotton Corporation and was used for spinning both American and Indian yarn. It was probably at this time that the name *Ark* was dropped in favour of *Welkin,* the name of the approach road. The mill had 78,680 spindles in use and employed up to 200 people in yarn production before closing in August 1962. A year later the firm of Buckley and Bland took over, primarily for printing Vernon's Pools Coupons. Buckley and Bland was established in 1881 by Harold Buckley and James Bland as printers and stationers, and were based in Manchester. The business developed, and by the time it relocated to Welkin Mill it was part owned by Vernon Sangster – hence the connection with the printing of pools coupons. Following in his father's footsteps Robert Sangster took control, but his interest in the breeding of race-horses took preference, and around 1982 Buckley and Bland became independent of Vernons Pools. In 1989 the firm became known simply as *Buckleys* and today holds its position as one of the U.K.'s leading colour printers, employing over 100 people supplying wet glue labels and general promotional print - mainly for the food and drink industries.

Information Sources:-
Bredbury – A Nostalgic History by Edna Reeves and John Turner

Cotton Mills in Greater Manchester – Mike Williams & D.A.Farnie

Wellington Mill

O.S.ref. SJ893 902

Wellington Mill was constructed in 1828 by Thomas Marsland, an established calico printer. At seven storeys high it was one of the tallest factories Stockport had seen until then, and it allowed Marsland to engage in spinning and weaving as well as printing and blue dying that he was well known for. By 1833 Marsland's workforce totalled 947, the largest in Stockport. Thomas Marsland (not to be confused with Peter Marsland of Woodbank Hall) became Tory M.P. for Stockport, serving from 1832 to 1841, and he was also a major in the militia. At about the same time as his election to parliament Thomas Marsland retired from the business, leaving it in the hands of relations, mainly sons-in-law Alexander Lingard and Richard Hole. A third son-in-law William Courteney Cruttenden also became involved in the business at a later date.

In 1874 the firm of J & G Walthew Ltd. took over the mill as cotton spinners and doublers, and for a time the premises were known as Walthew's Mill. John and George Walthew also operated two other mills in Stockport, known as 'Spring Mount' and 'Brinksway' respectively.

In 1895 Ward Brothers (Hatting) moved into Wellington Mill from Bredbury, where they had been established for 40 years. They left their mark for all to see by having the words WARD BROS "W" MAKE HATS painted on the brickwork of the lift tower. This was obliterated in 1997 when the upper floors were refurbished and converted into flats. Ward Bros. were in business at Wellington Mill until 1935. The premises were under utilised for many years before the refurbishment but will be remembered by many as a warehouse for a cycle distributor. Appropriately Stockport Metropolitan Borough Council came forward with a rescue plan to preserve both the premises and the memory of hat making in the borough by creating the U.K.'s first and only Museum of Hatting at Wellington Mill. The so-called *Hat Works Museum* was opened on 24th April 2000 and occupies the lower three floors of this Grade II listed building. The top floors of the building were refurbished and converted into what was described as '46 superb apartments.'

Stockport during the Industrial Revolution (c 1845)

When the mill was built it was virtually unique by way of construction in having cast iron roof trusses as well as cast iron beams and columns. It remains therefore as one of the best surviving examples of an early "fireproof mill". The attic formed by the space below the roof trusses is lit by a lunette set in the west gable. It is thought that the chimney was added at a later date from the main building – probably in the 1860's. It is taller than it appears from a distance as it rises from a level lower than the entrance to the building, and is about 200ft. tall overall. It was re-pointed in 1998 and later dressed on two sides to advertise the Hat Museum. Today the chimney is a landmark in Stockport and is one of the few remaining from the 19th century to remind us of our industrial heritage.

150 years later – Wellington Mill from Daw Bank

Information Sources:- *Stockport : A History* by Peter Arrowsmith
Industrial Archaeology of Stockport by Owen Ashmore

BLANK PAGE

INDEX